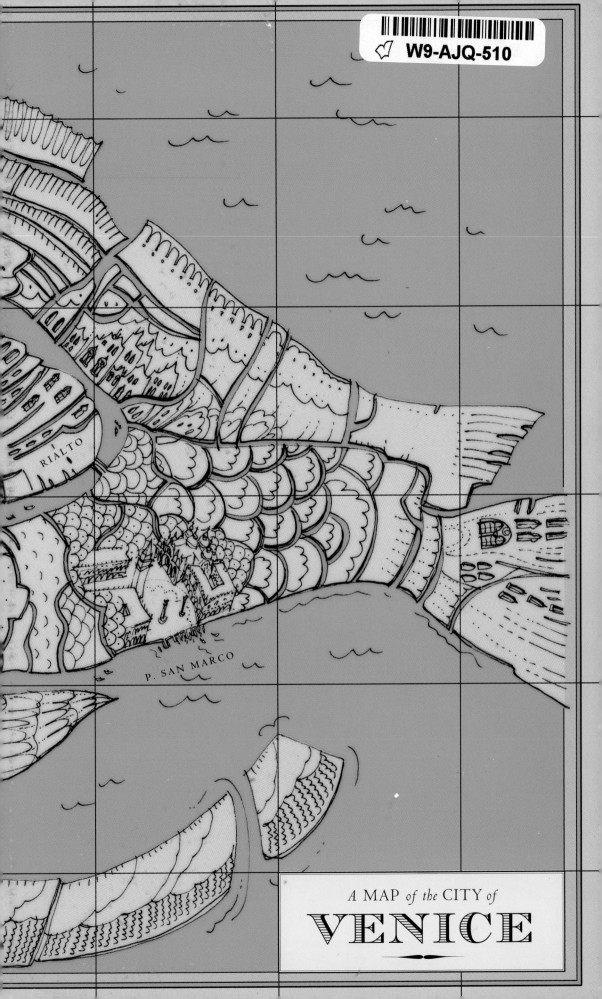

RIALTO

P. SAN MARCO

A MAP of the CITY of

# VENICE

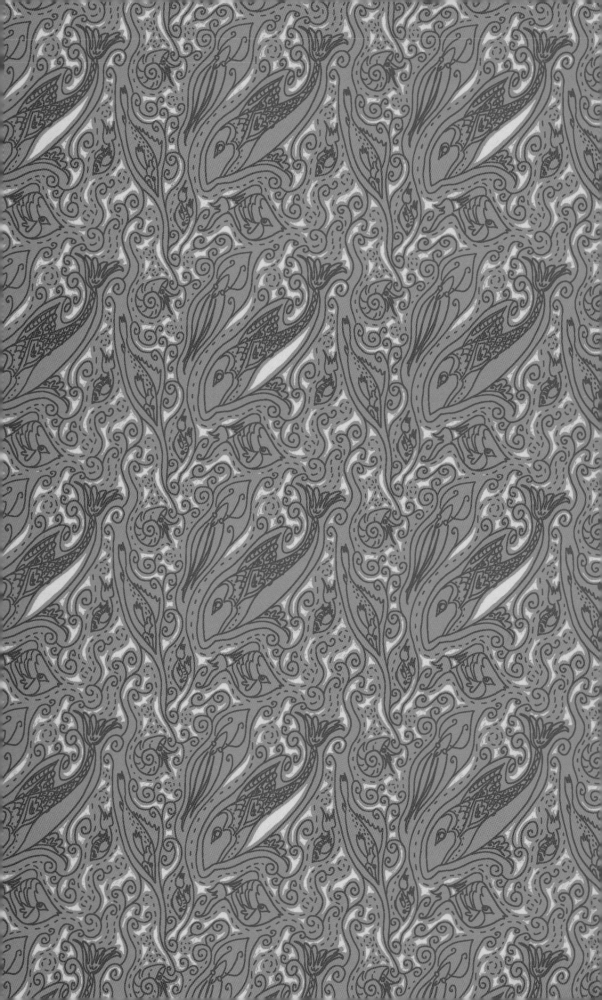

# The
# MERCHANT
## of
# VENICE

a play by William Shakespeare

adapted and illustrated by Gareth Hinds

CANDLEWICK PRESS
CAMBRIDGE, MASSACHUSETTS

# DRAMATIS PERSONAE

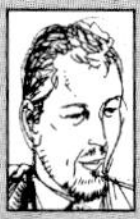

ANTONIO ........ *a merchant of Venice*

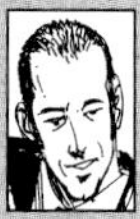

BASSANIO ........ *his friend, suitor to Portia*

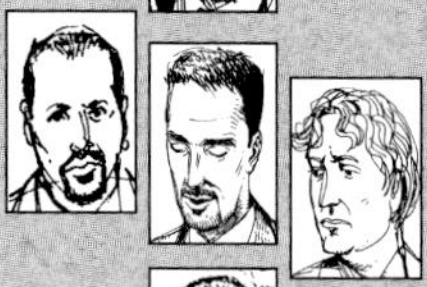

GRATIANO, SALERIO, SALANIO ........ *friends to Antonio and Bassanio*

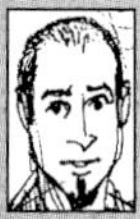

LORENZO ........ *in love with Jessica*

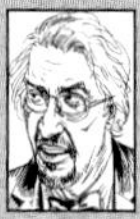

SHYLOCK ........ *a rich Jew*

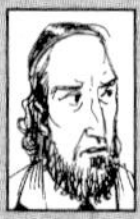

TUBAL ........ *a Jew, his friend*

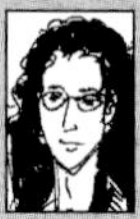

JESSICA ........ *daughter to Shylock*

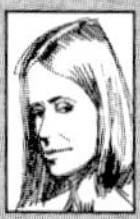

PORTIA ........ *a rich heiress*

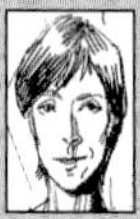

NERISSA ........ *her waiting-maid*

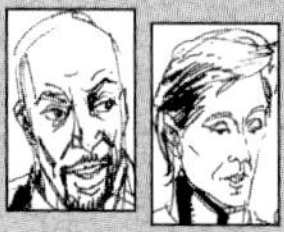

The Prince of MOROCCO, ........ *suitors to Portia*
The Prince of ARAGON

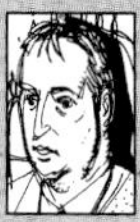

The Duke of VENICE

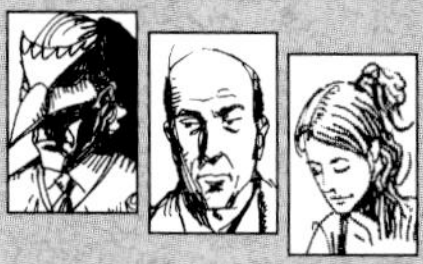

*Magnificoes of Venice; officers of the Court of Justice;*
*servants to Portia; and other attendants*

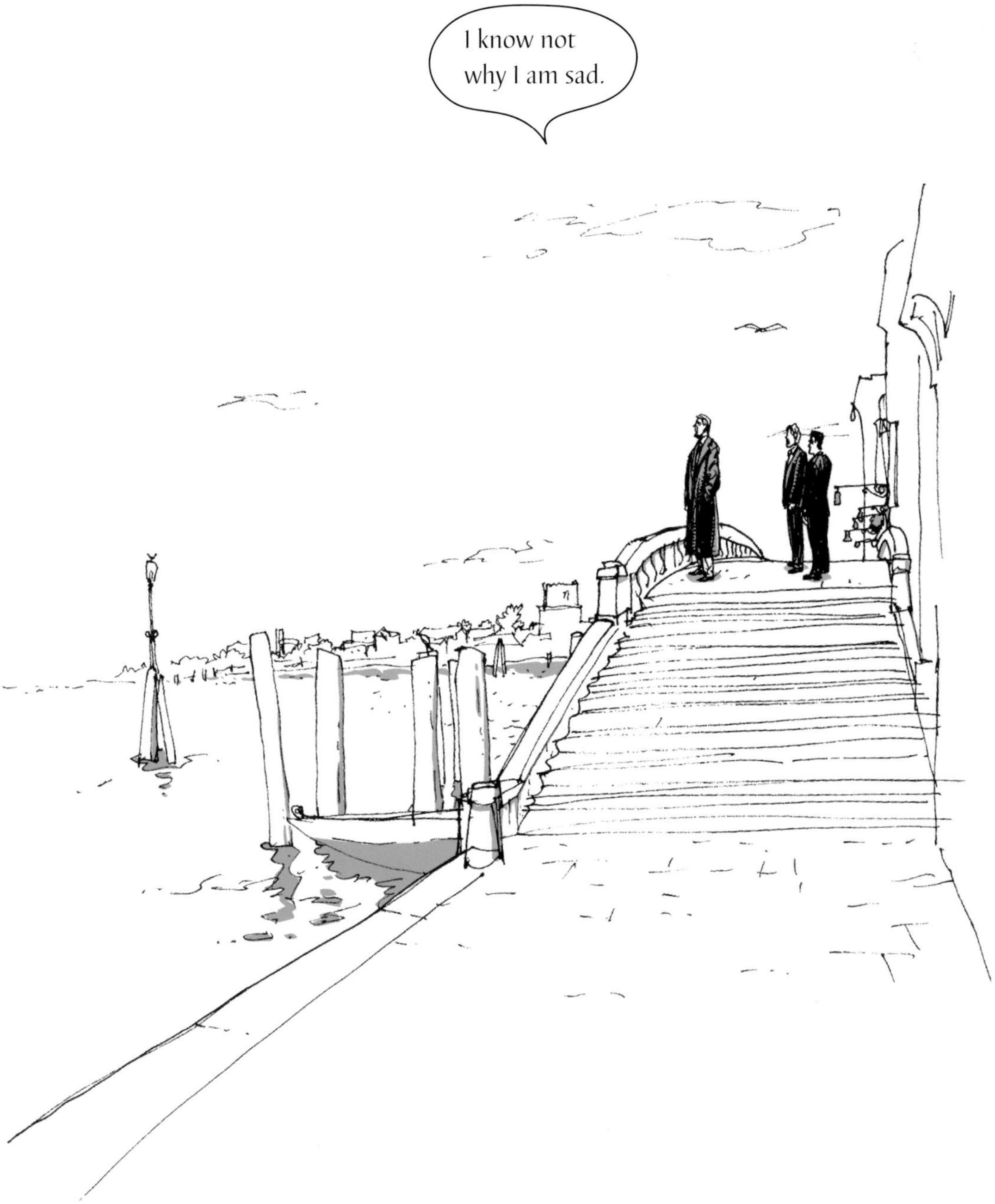
I know not
why I am sad.

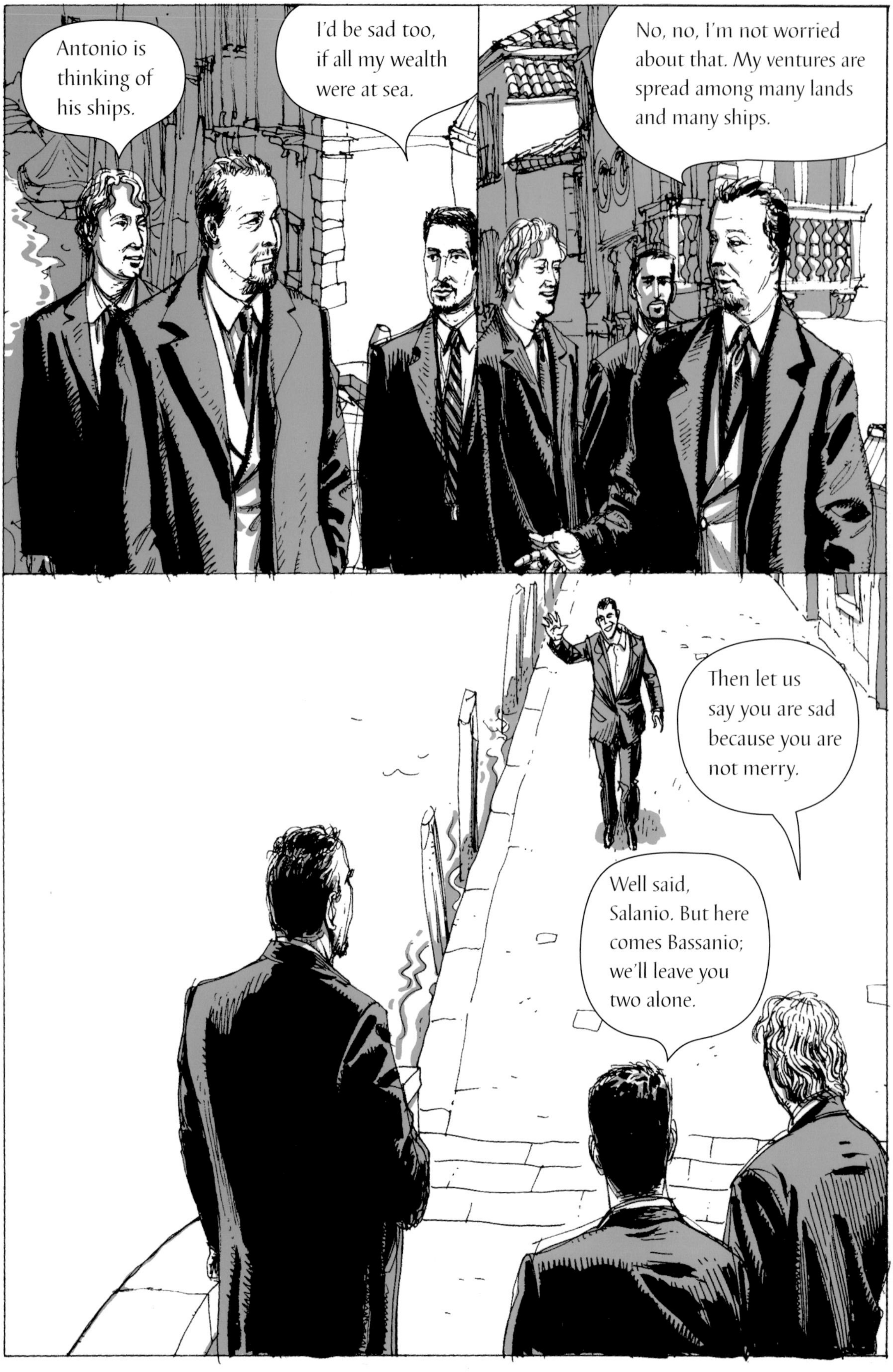
Antonio is thinking of his ships.
I'd be sad too, if all my wealth were at sea.
No, no, I'm not worried about that. My ventures are spread among many lands and many ships.
Then let us say you are sad because you are not merry.
Well said, Salanio. But here comes Bassanio; we'll leave you two alone.

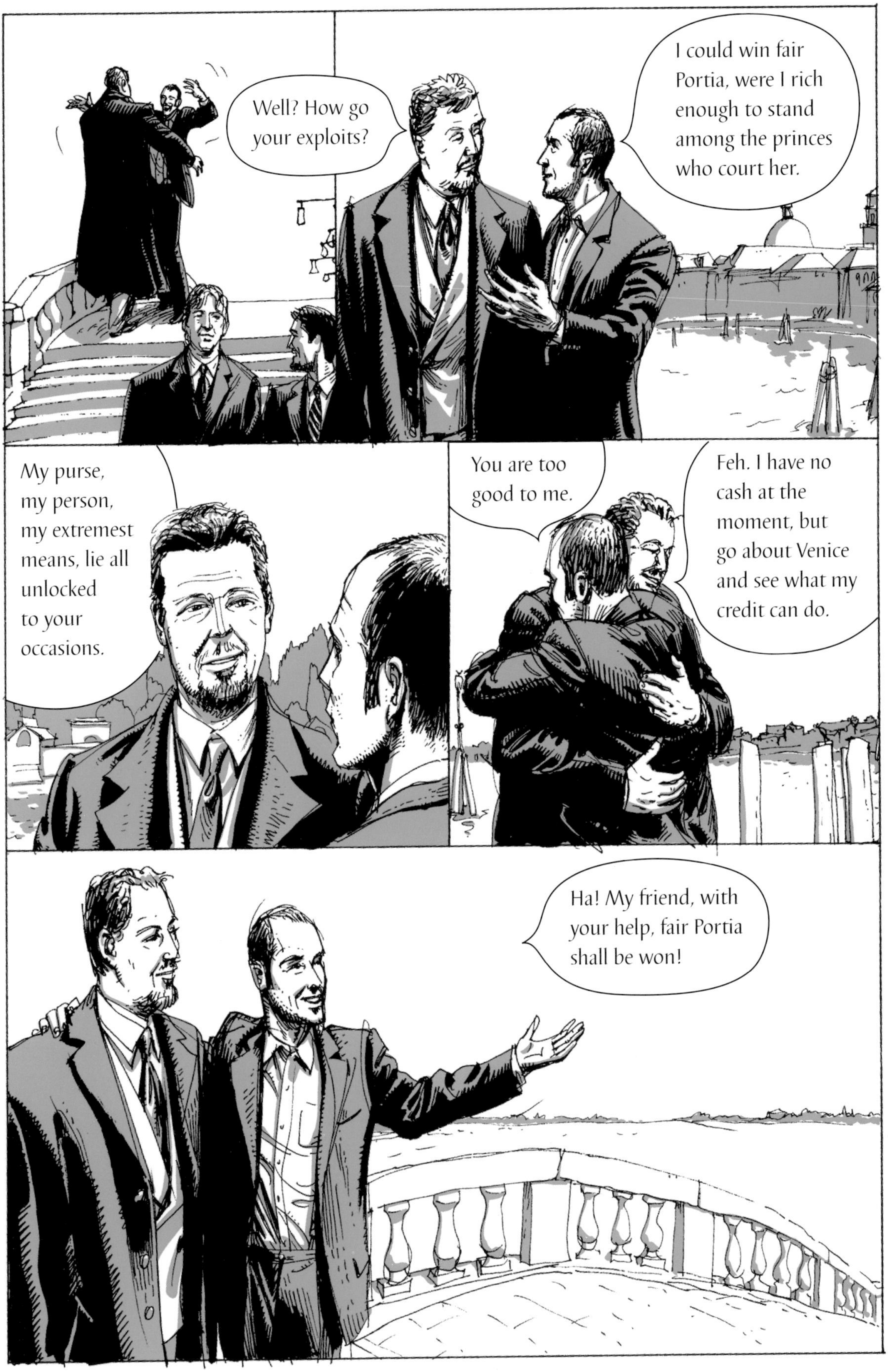
Well? How go your exploits?
I could win fair Portia, were I rich enough to stand among the princes who court her.
My purse, my person, my extremest means, lie all unlocked to your occasions.
You are too good to me.
Feh. I have no cash at the moment, but go about Venice and see what my credit can do.
Ha! My friend, with your help, fair Portia shall be won!

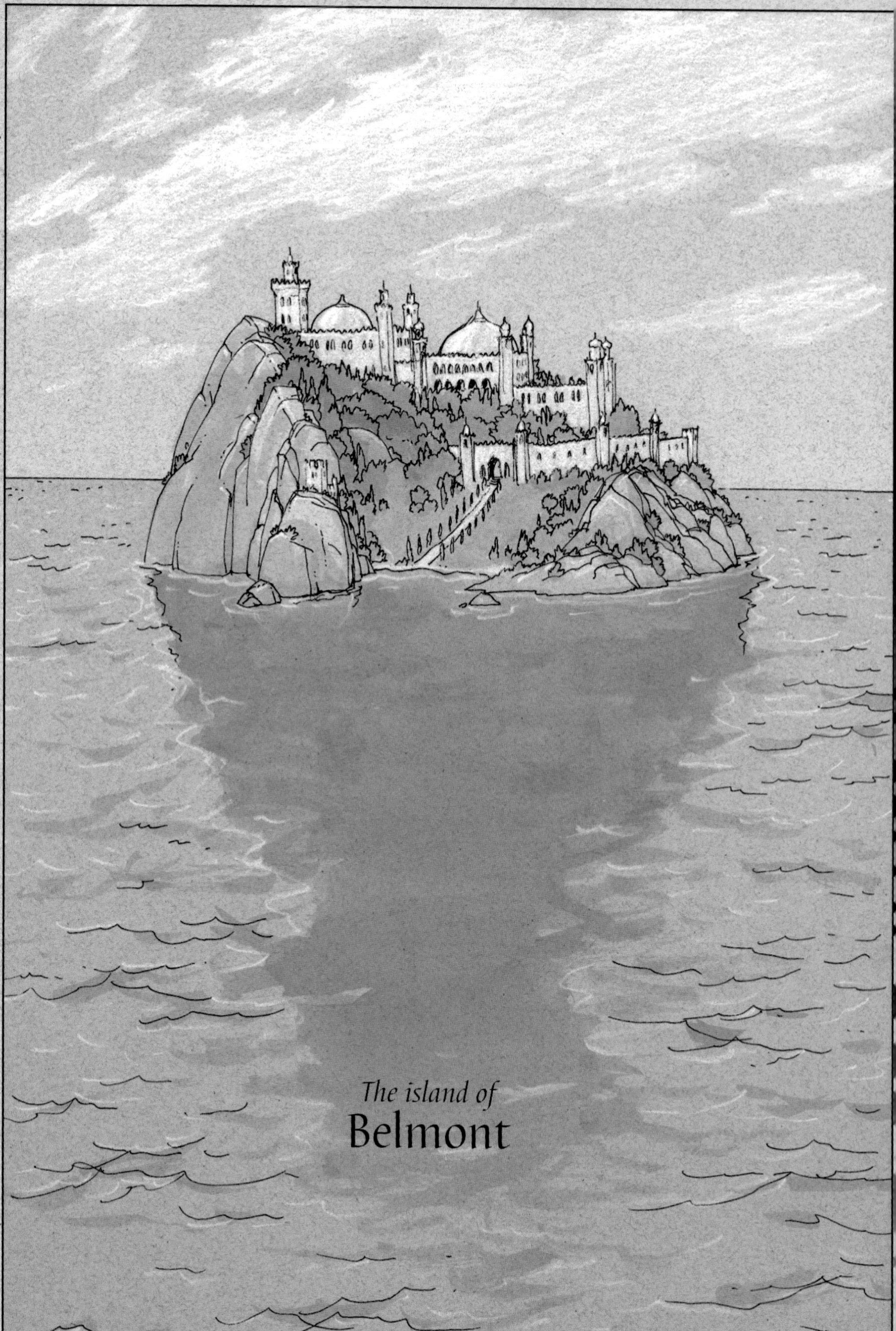
The island of
Belmont

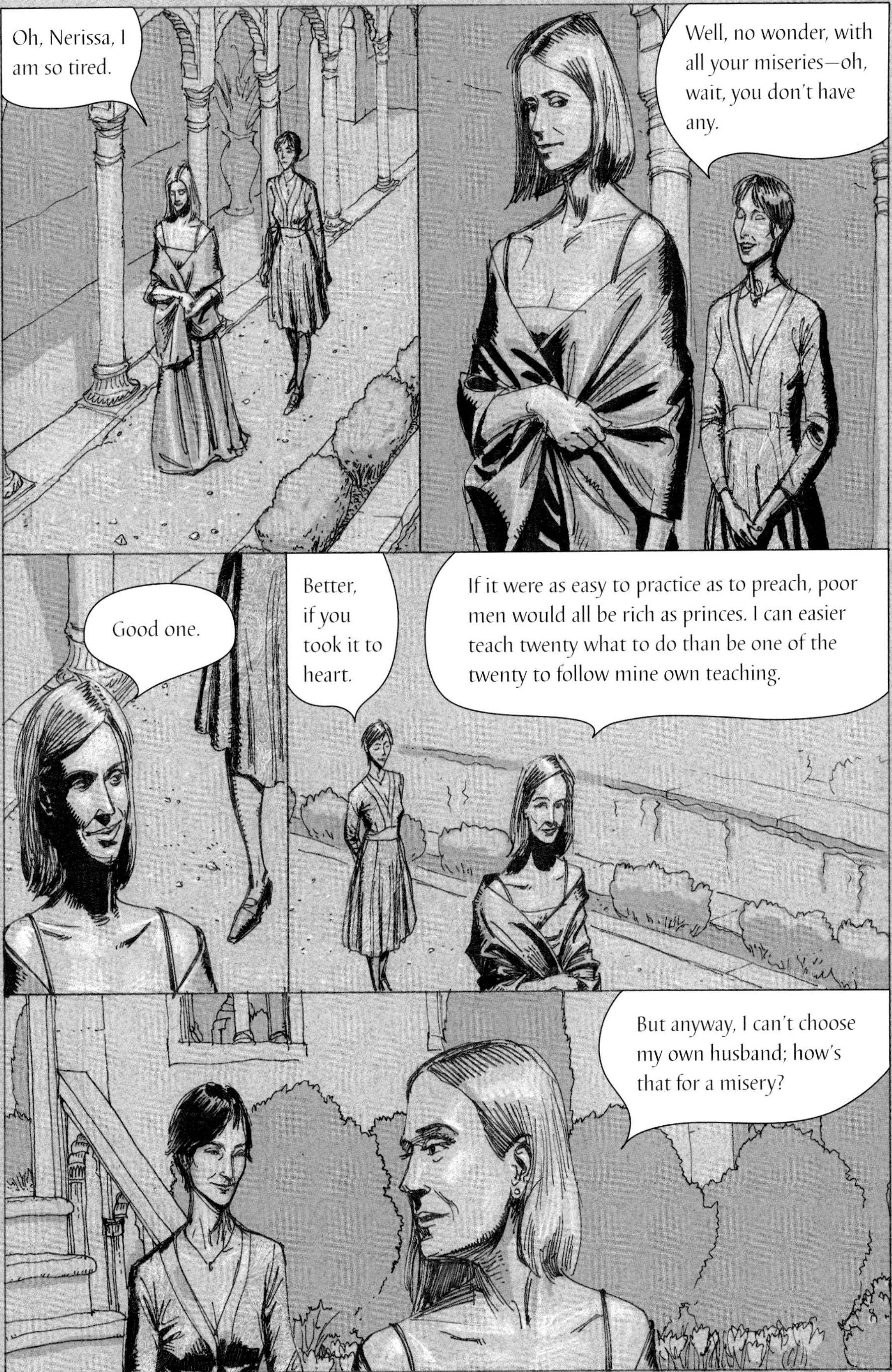
Oh, Nerissa, I am so tired.
Well, no wonder, with all your miseries—oh, wait, you don't have any.
Good one.
Better, if you took it to heart.
If it were as easy to practice as to preach, poor men would all be rich as princes. I can easier teach twenty what to do than be one of the twenty to follow mine own teaching.
But anyway, I can't choose my own husband; how's that for a misery?

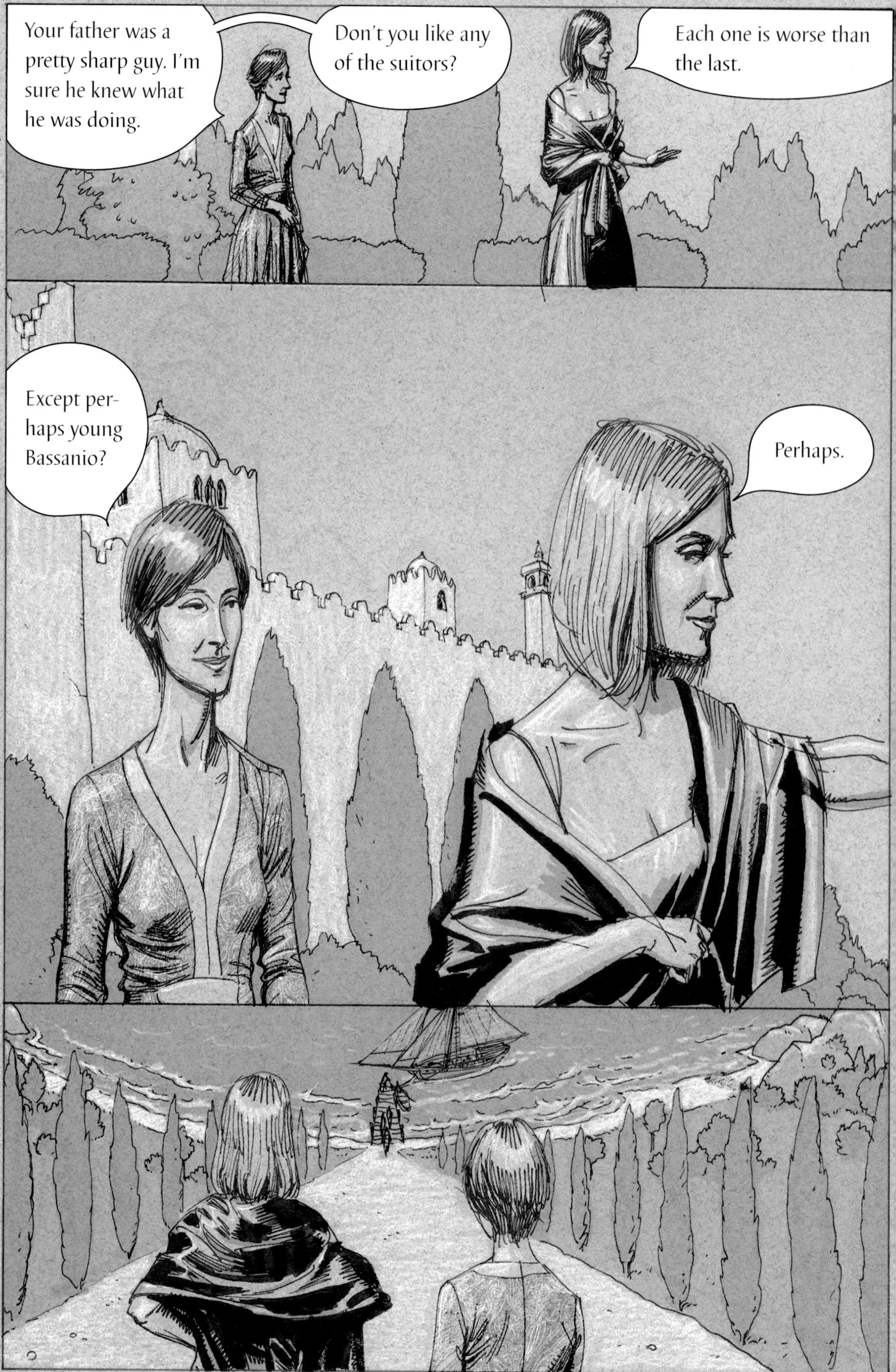

Your father was a pretty sharp guy. I'm sure he knew what he was doing.
Don't you like any of the suitors?
Each one is worse than the last.
Except perhaps young Bassanio?
Perhaps.

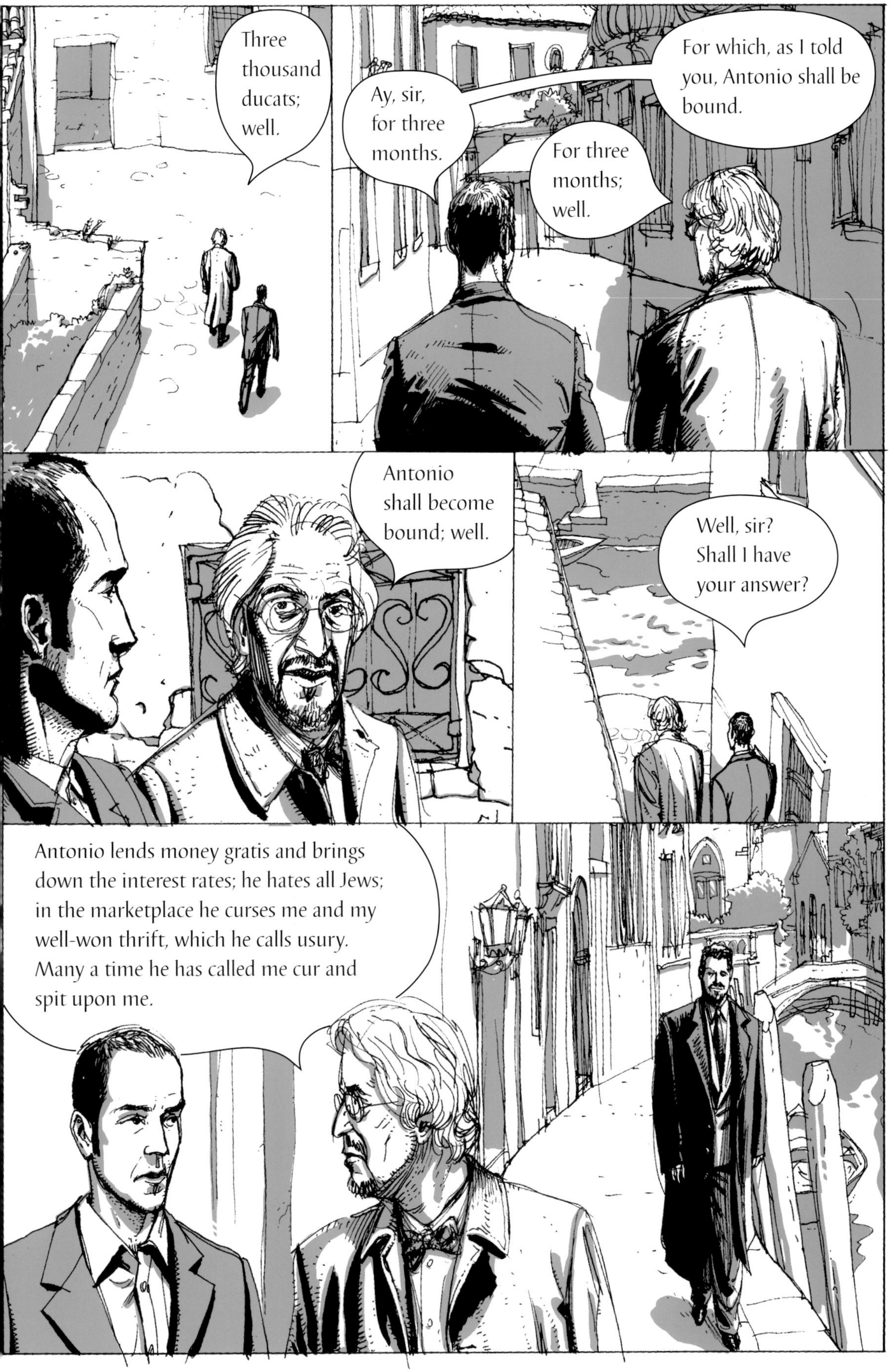
Three thousand ducats; well.
Ay, sir, for three months.
For which, as I told you, Antonio shall be bound.
For three months; well.
Antonio shall become bound; well.
Well, sir? Shall I have your answer?
Antonio lends money gratis and brings down the interest rates; he hates all Jews; in the marketplace he curses me and my well-won thrift, which he calls usury. Many a time he has called me cur and spit upon me.

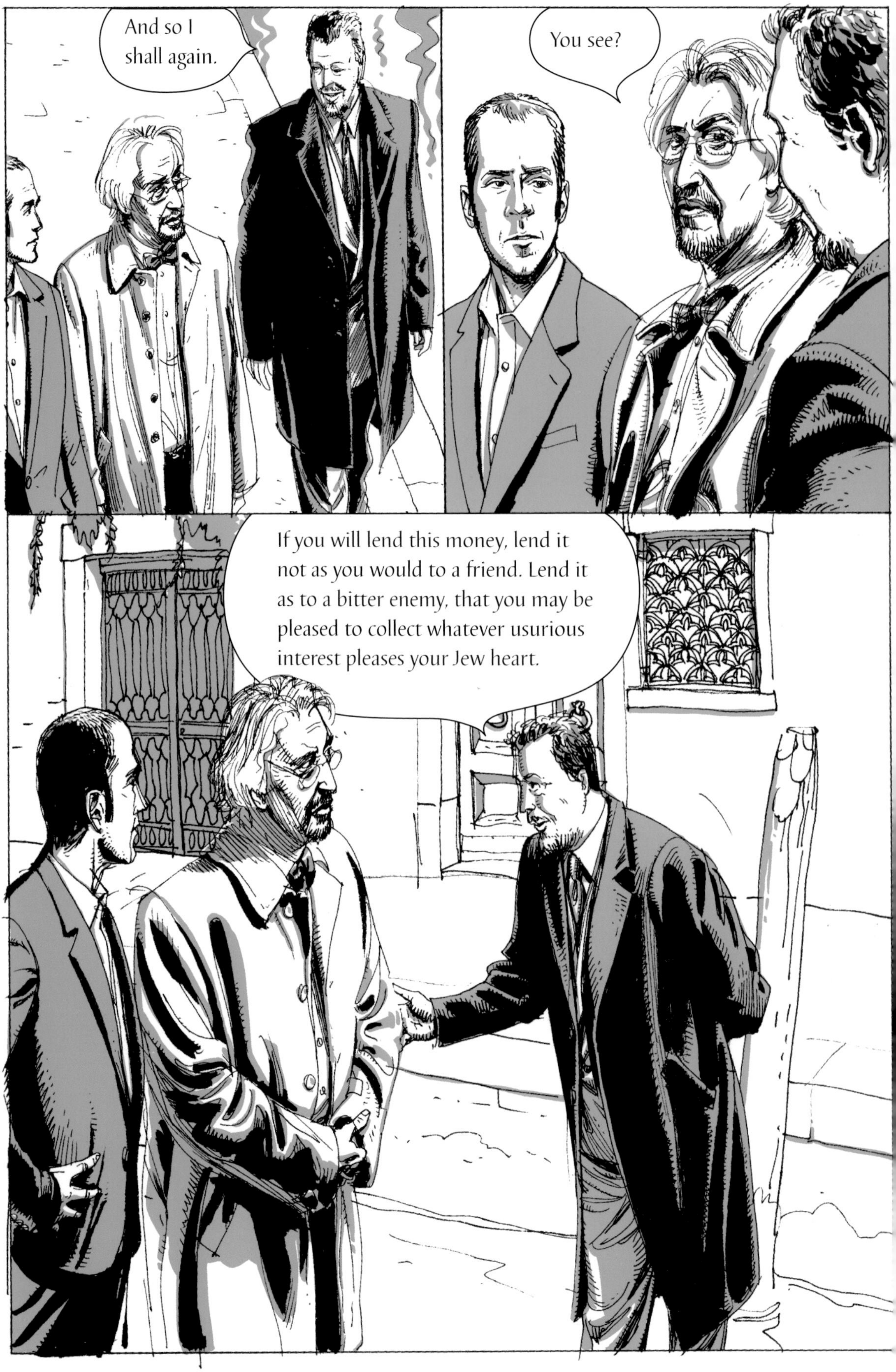
And so I shall again.
You see?
If you will lend this money, lend it not as you would to a friend. Lend it as to a bitter enemy, that you may be pleased to collect whatever usurious interest pleases your Jew heart.

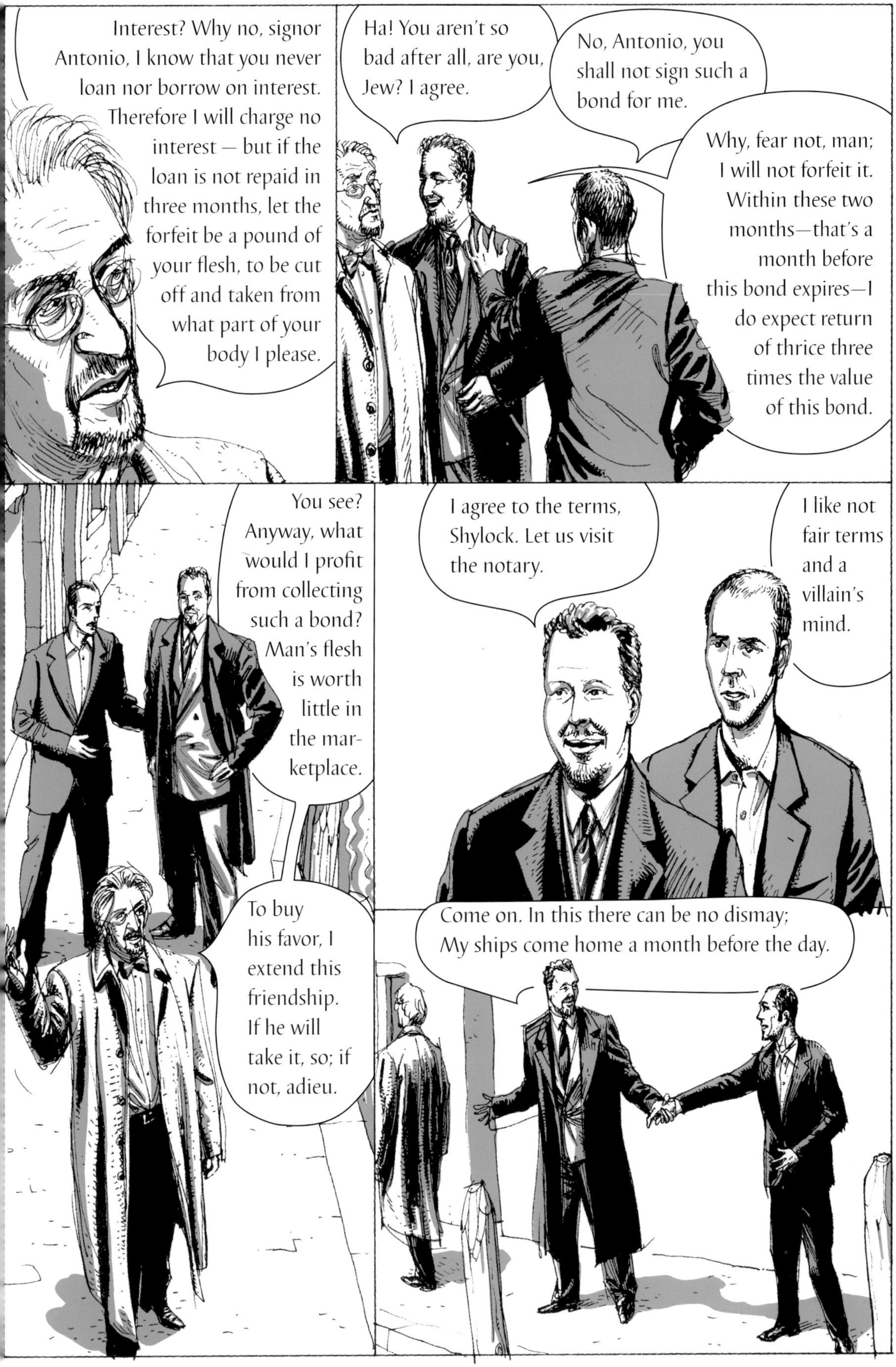
Interest? Why no, signor Antonio, I know that you never loan nor borrow on interest. Therefore I will charge no interest — but if the loan is not repaid in three months, let the forfeit be a pound of your flesh, to be cut off and taken from what part of your body I please.
Ha! You aren't so bad after all, are you, Jew? I agree.
No, Antonio, you shall not sign such a bond for me.
Why, fear not, man; I will not forfeit it. Within these two months—that's a month before this bond expires—I do expect return of thrice three times the value of this bond.
You see? Anyway, what would I profit from collecting such a bond? Man's flesh is worth little in the mar-ketplace.
To buy his favor, I extend this friendship. If he will take it, so; if not, adieu.
I agree to the terms, Shylock. Let us visit the notary.
I like not fair terms and a villain's mind.
Come on. In this there can be no dismay;
My ships come home a month before the day.

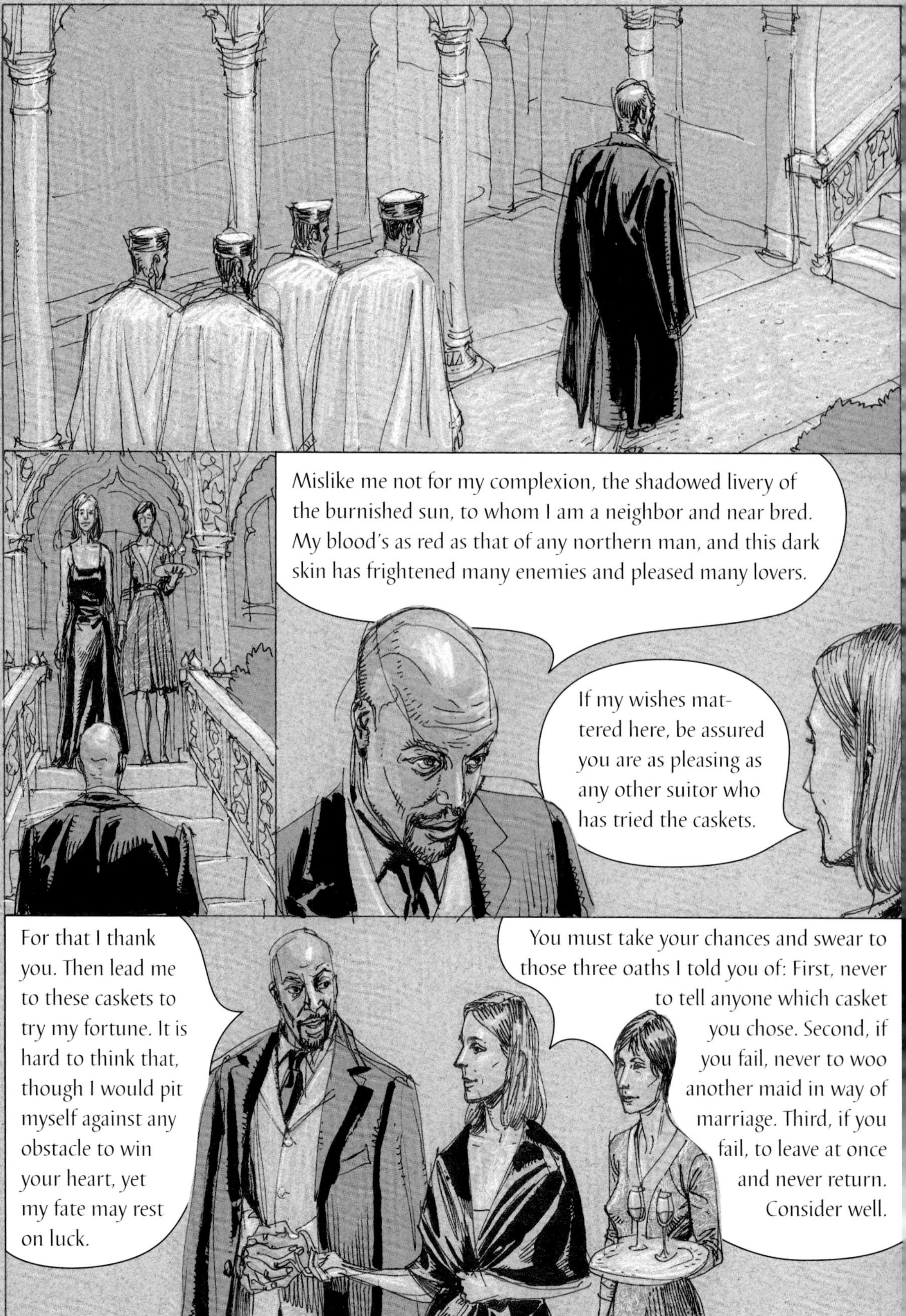
Mislike me not for my complexion, the shadowed livery of the burnished sun, to whom I am a neighbor and near bred. My blood's as red as that of any northern man, and this dark skin has frightened many enemies and pleased many lovers.
If my wishes mattered here, be assured you are as pleasing as any other suitor who has tried the caskets.
For that I thank you. Then lead me to these caskets to try my fortune. It is hard to think that, though I would pit myself against any obstacle to win your heart, yet my fate may rest on luck.
You must take your chances and swear to those three oaths I told you of: First, never to tell anyone which casket you chose. Second, if you fail, never to woo another maid in way of marriage. Third, if you fail, to leave at once and never return. Consider well.

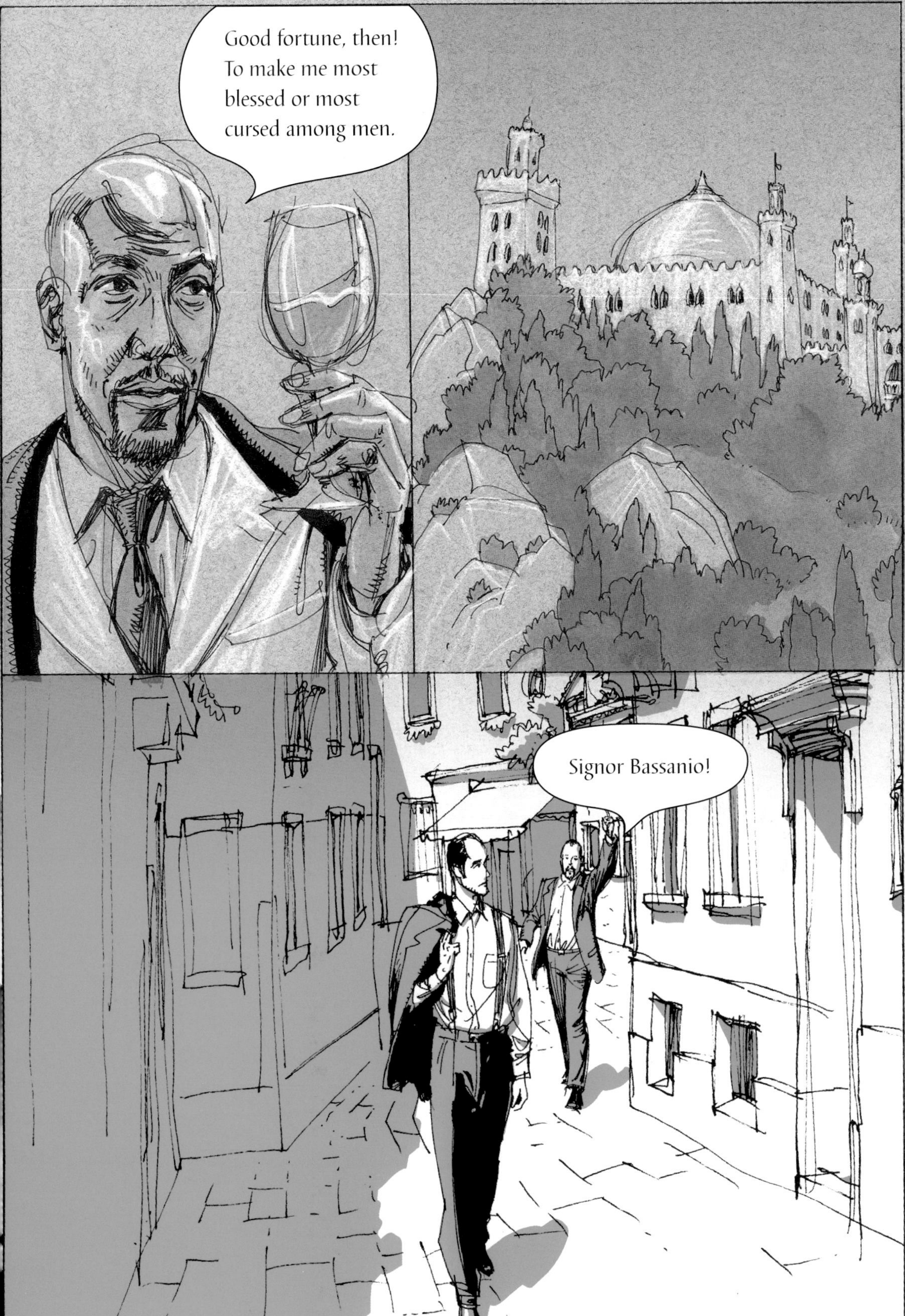
Good fortune, then! To make me most blessed or most cursed among men.
Signor Bassanio!
Act II, scene 2

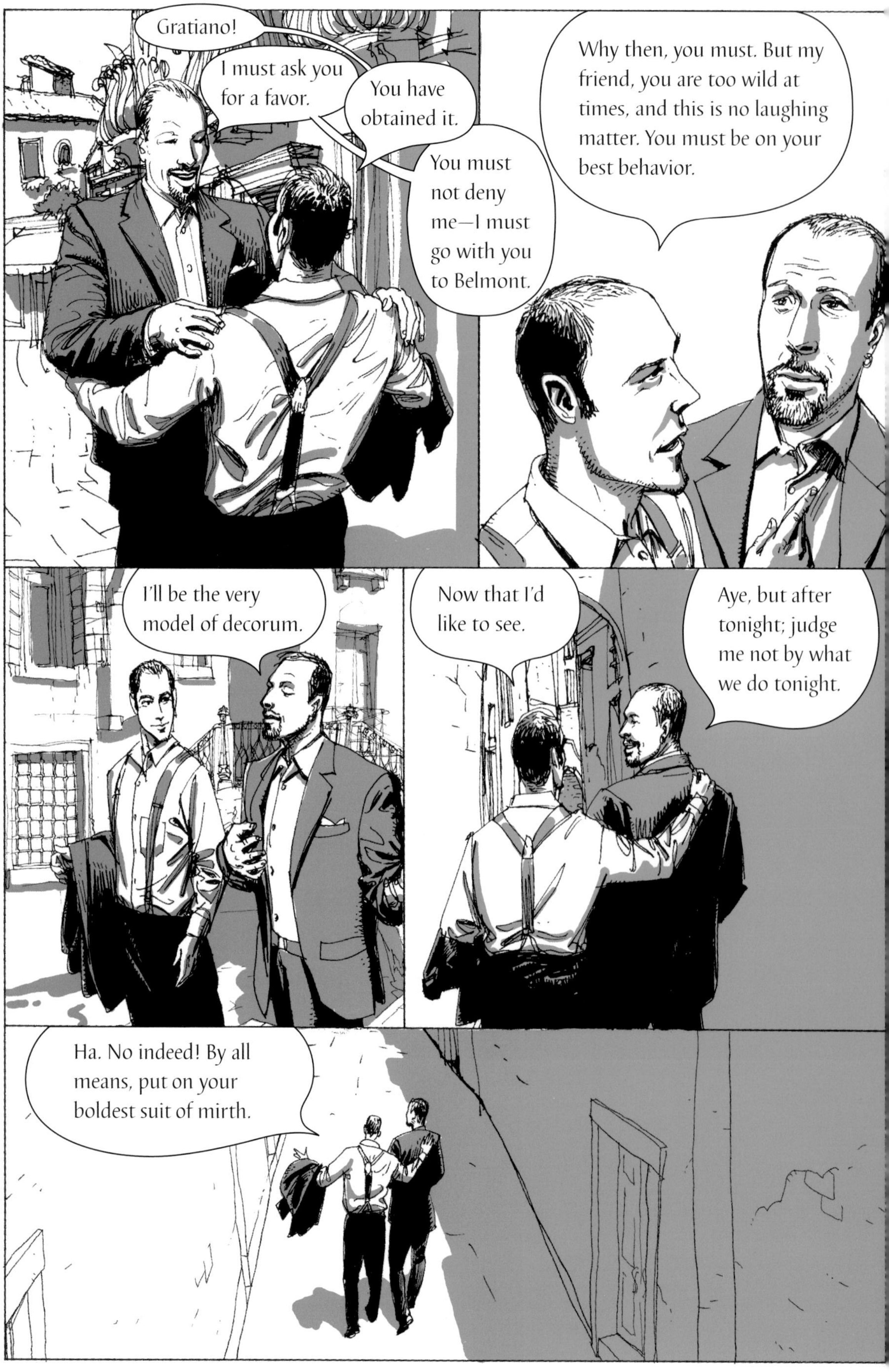
Gratiano!
I must ask you for a favor.
You have obtained it.
You must not deny me—I must go with you to Belmont.
Why then, you must. But my friend, you are too wild at times, and this is no laughing matter. You must be on your best behavior.
I'll be the very model of decorum.
Now that I'd like to see.
Aye, but after tonight; judge me not by what we do tonight.
Ha. No indeed! By all means, put on your boldest suit of mirth.

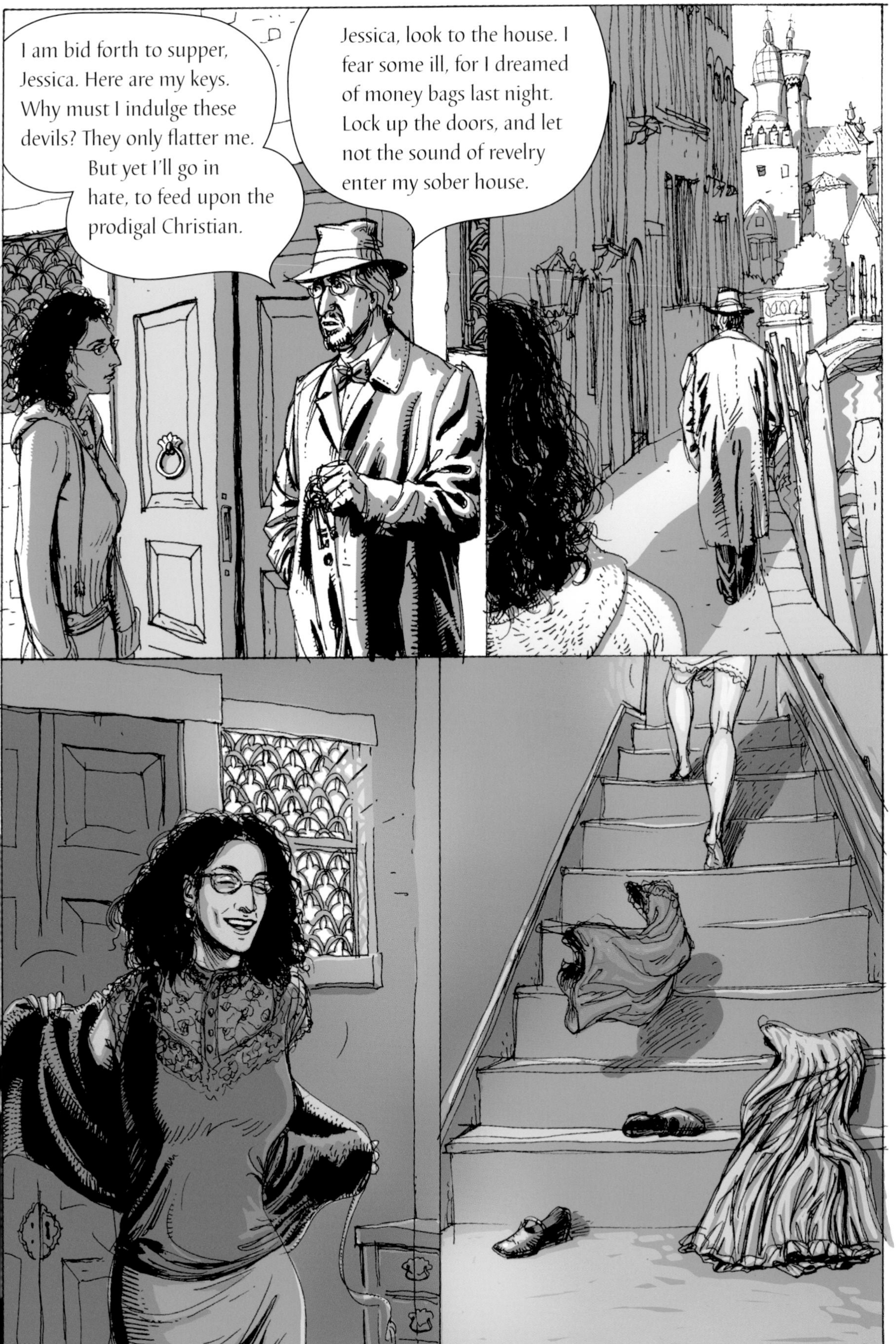
I am bid forth to supper, Jessica. Here are my keys. Why must I indulge these devils? They only flatter me. But yet I'll go in hate, to feed upon the prodigal Christian.
Jessica, look to the house. I fear some ill, for I dreamed of money bags last night. Lock up the doors, and let not the sound of revelry enter my sober house.

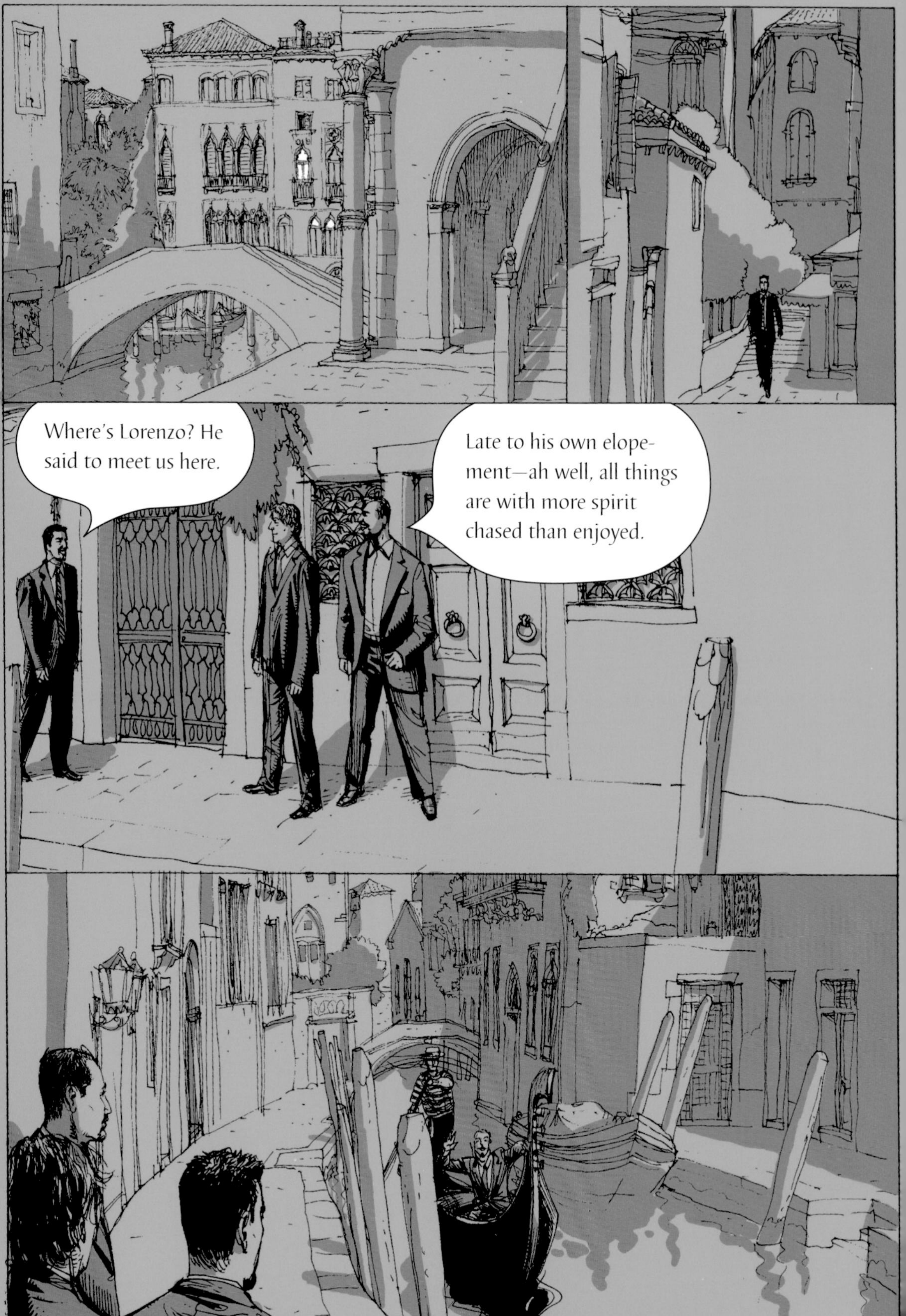
Where's Lorenzo? He said to meet us here.
Late to his own elopement—ah well, all things are with more spirit chased than enjoyed.

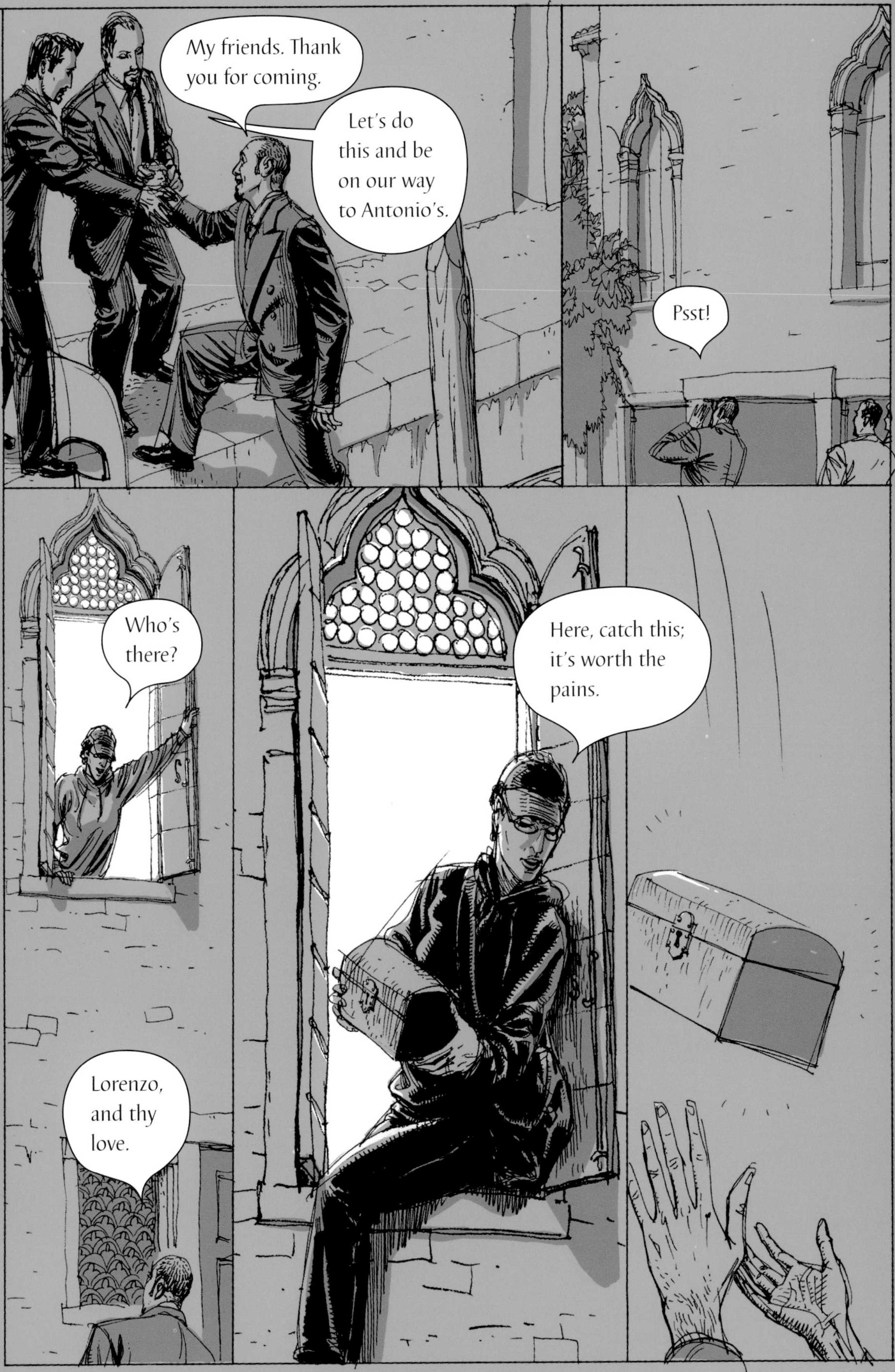
My friends. Thank you for coming.
Let's do this and be on our way to Antonio's.
Psst!
Who's there?
Lorenzo, and thy love.
Here, catch this; it's worth the pains.

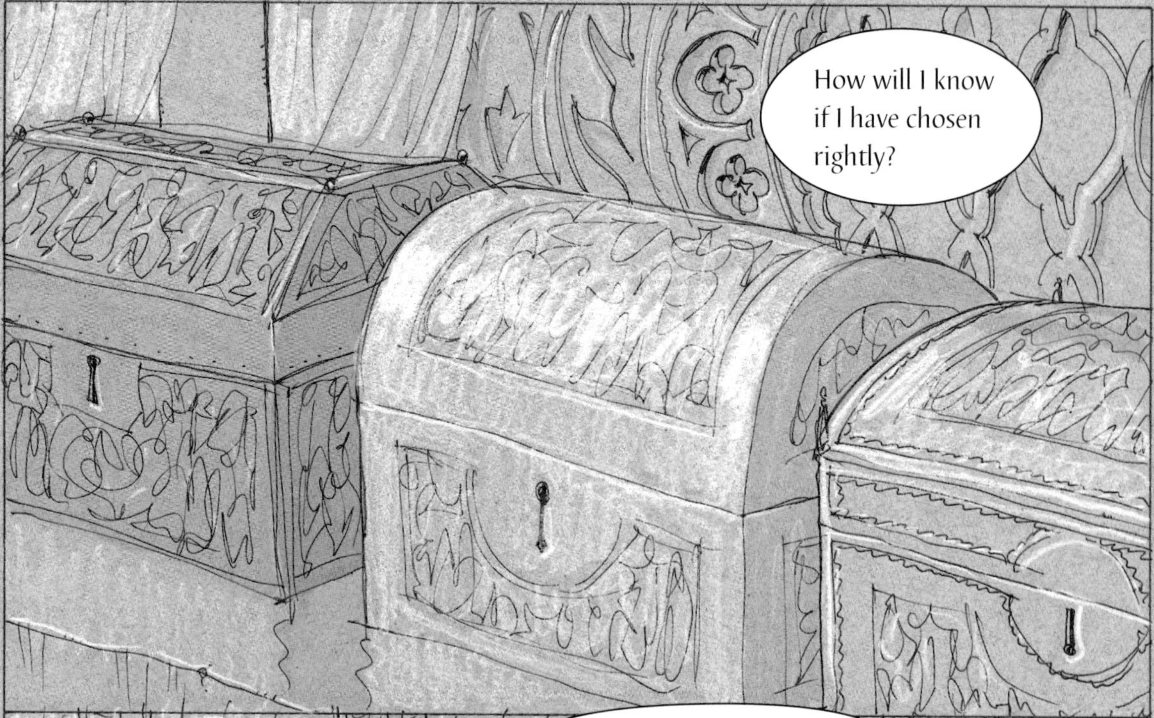
How will I know if I have chosen rightly?

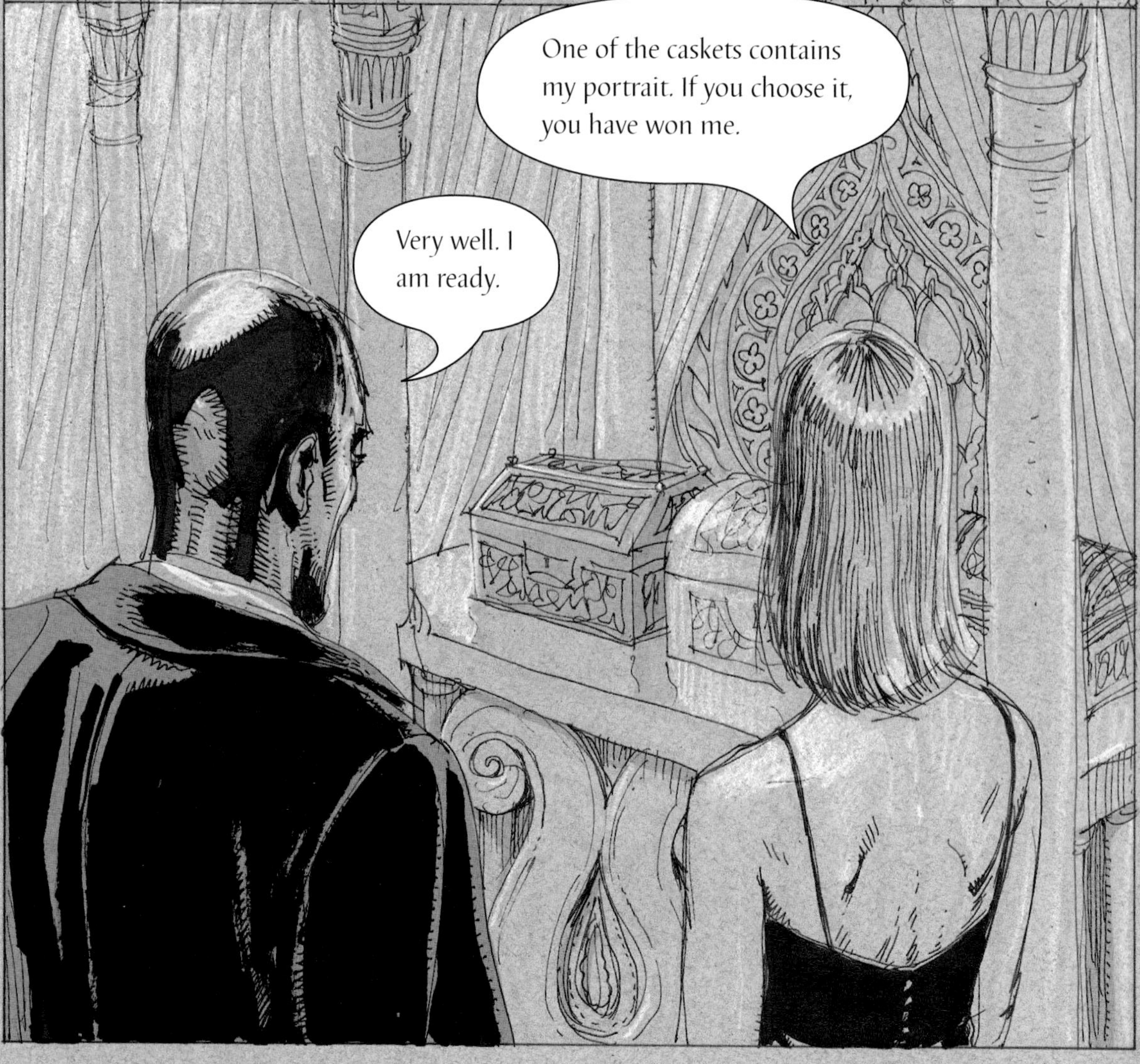
One of the caskets contains my portrait. If you choose it, you have won me.
Very well. I am ready.

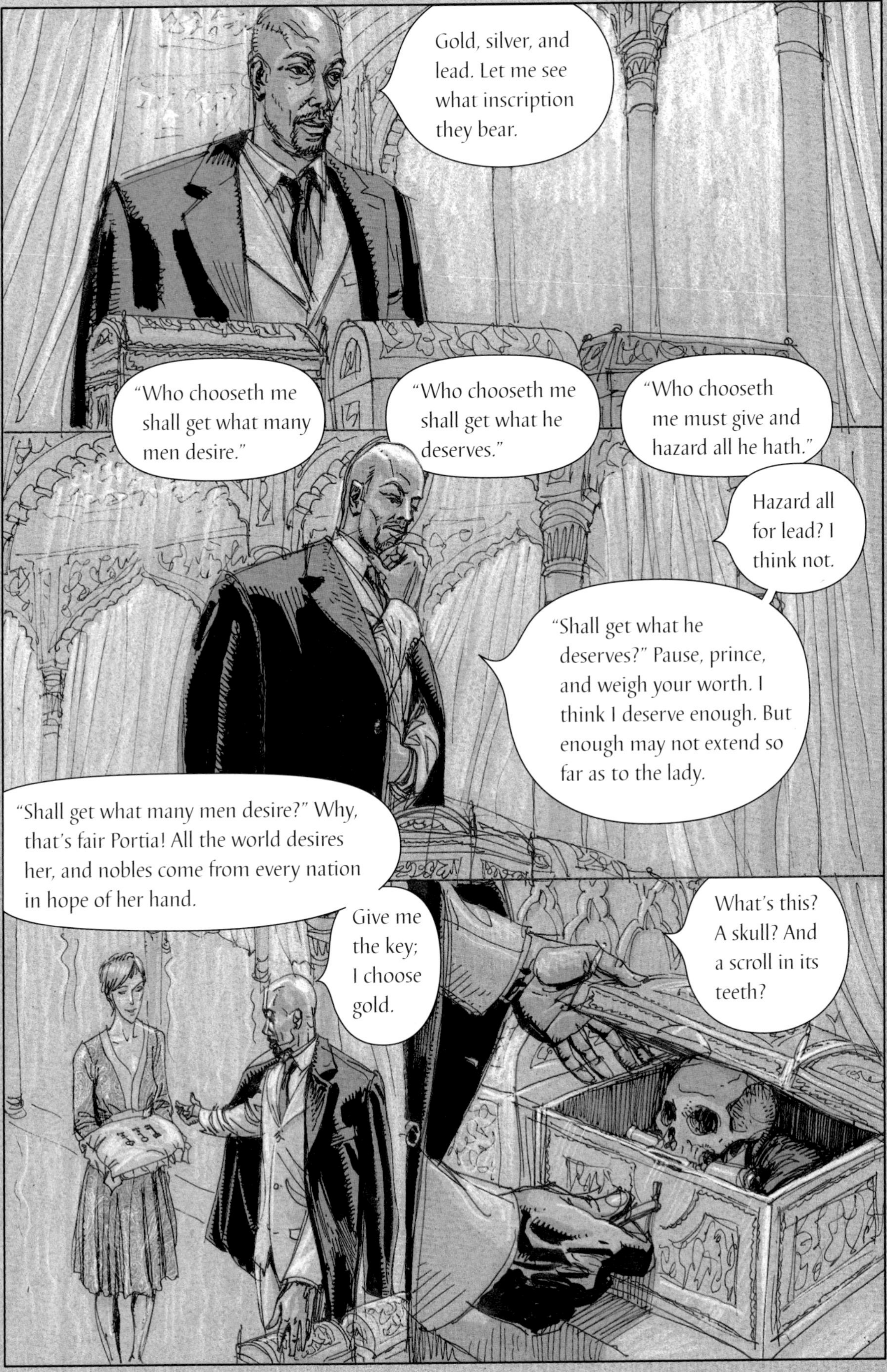
Gold, silver, and lead. Let me see what inscription they bear.
"Who chooseth me shall get what many men desire."
"Who chooseth me shall get what he deserves."
"Who chooseth me must give and hazard all he hath."
Hazard all for lead? I think not.
"Shall get what he deserves?" Pause, prince, and weigh your worth. I think I deserve enough. But enough may not extend so far as to the lady.
"Shall get what many men desire?" Why, that's fair Portia! All the world desires her, and nobles come from every nation in hope of her hand.
Give me the key; I choose gold.
What's this? A skull? And a scroll in its teeth?

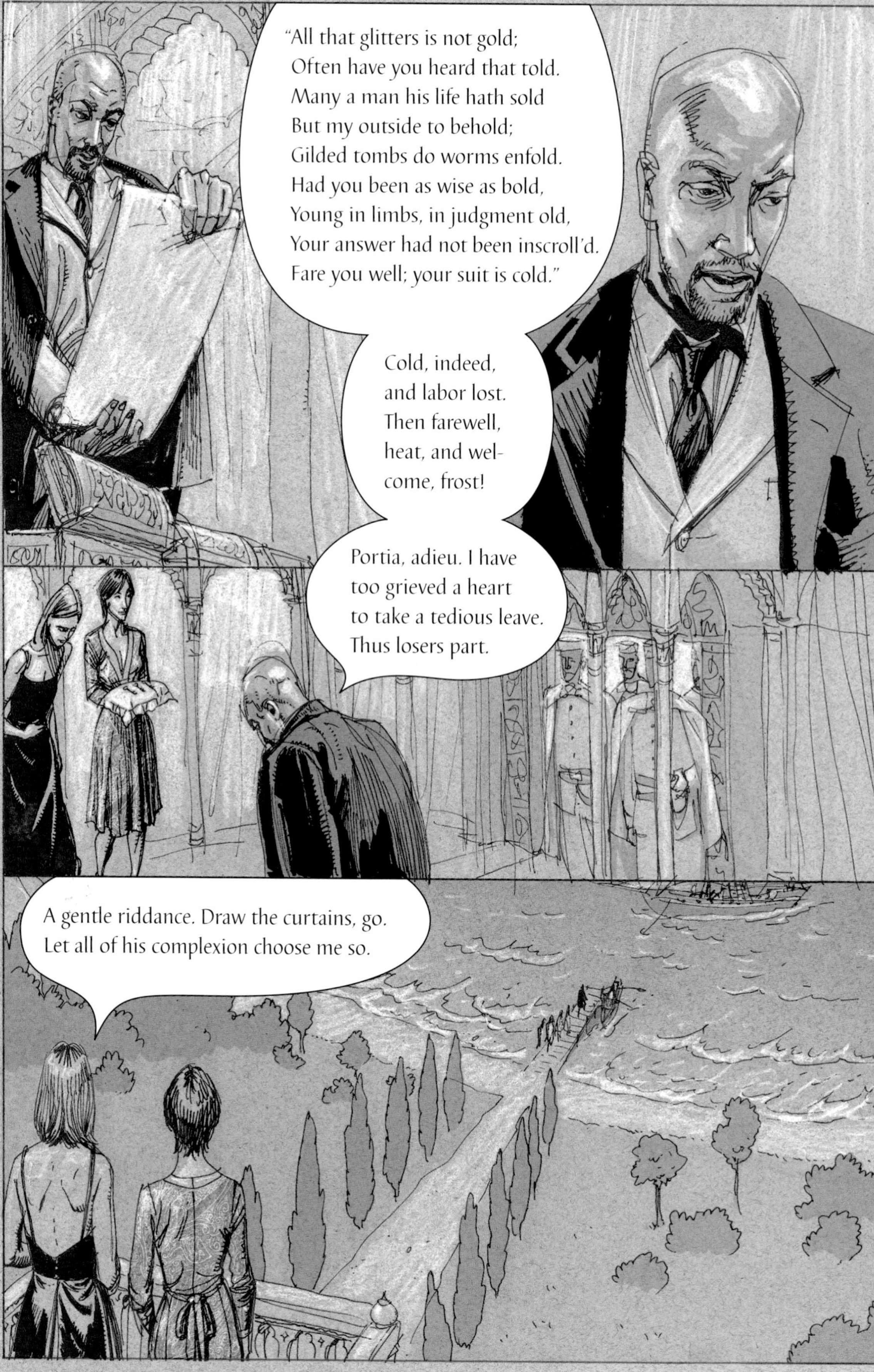
"All that glitters is not gold;
Often have you heard that told.
Many a man his life hath sold
But my outside to behold;
Gilded tombs do worms enfold.
Had you been as wise as bold,
Young in limbs, in judgment old,
Your answer had not been inscroll'd.
Fare you well; your suit is cold."
Cold, indeed, and labor lost. Then farewell, heat, and wel-come, frost!
Portia, adieu. I have too grieved a heart to take a tedious leave. Thus losers part.
A gentle riddance. Draw the curtains, go. Let all of his complexion choose me so.

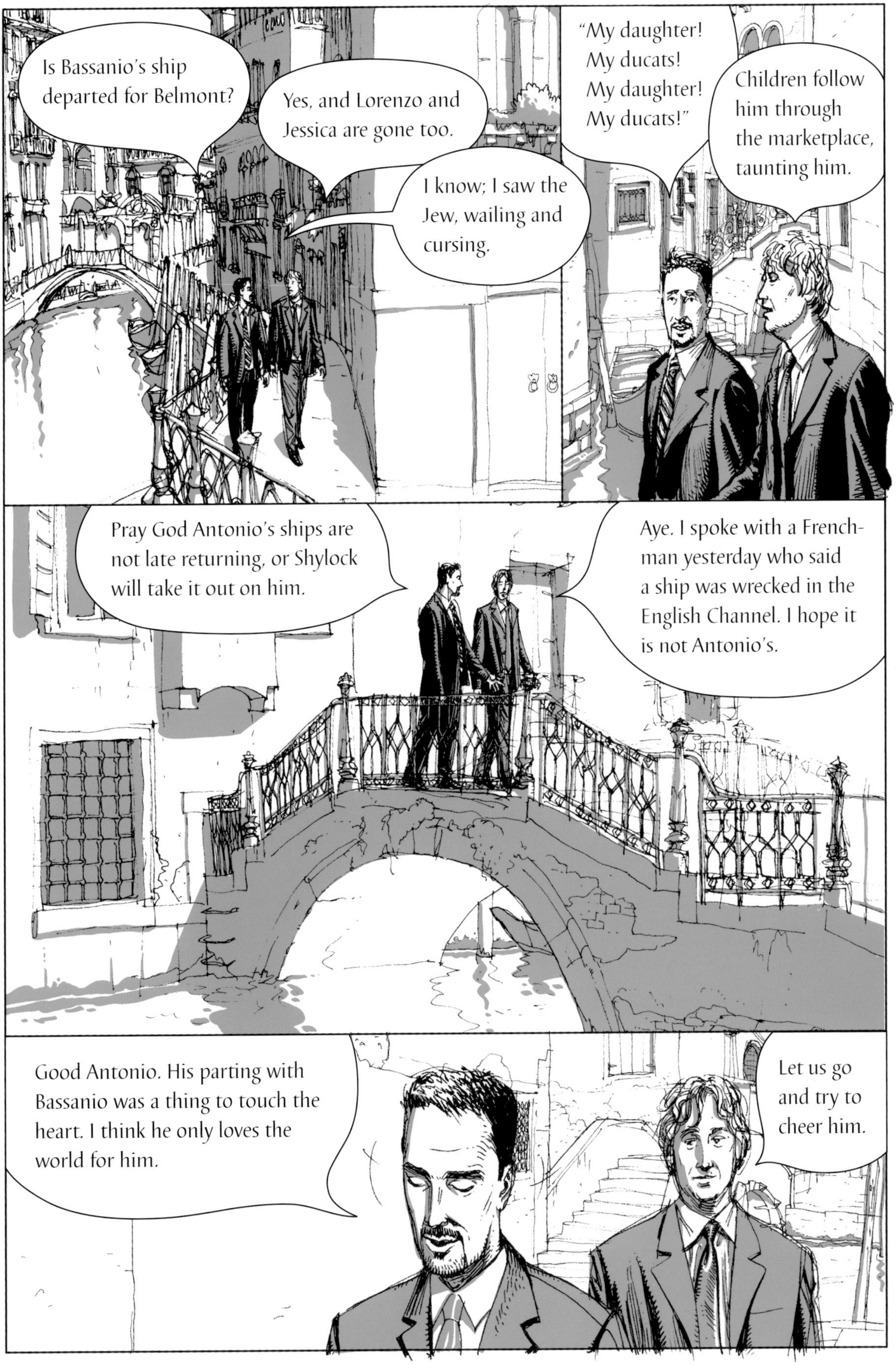
Is Bassanio's ship departed for Belmont?
Yes, and Lorenzo and Jessica are gone too.
I know; I saw the Jew, wailing and cursing.
"My daughter! My ducats! My daughter! My ducats!"
Children follow him through the marketplace, taunting him.
Pray God Antonio's ships are not late returning, or Shylock will take it out on him.
Aye. I spoke with a Frenchman yesterday who said a ship was wrecked in the English Channel. I hope it is not Antonio's.
Good Antonio. His parting with Bassanio was a thing to touch the heart. I think he only loves the world for him.
Let us go and try to cheer him.

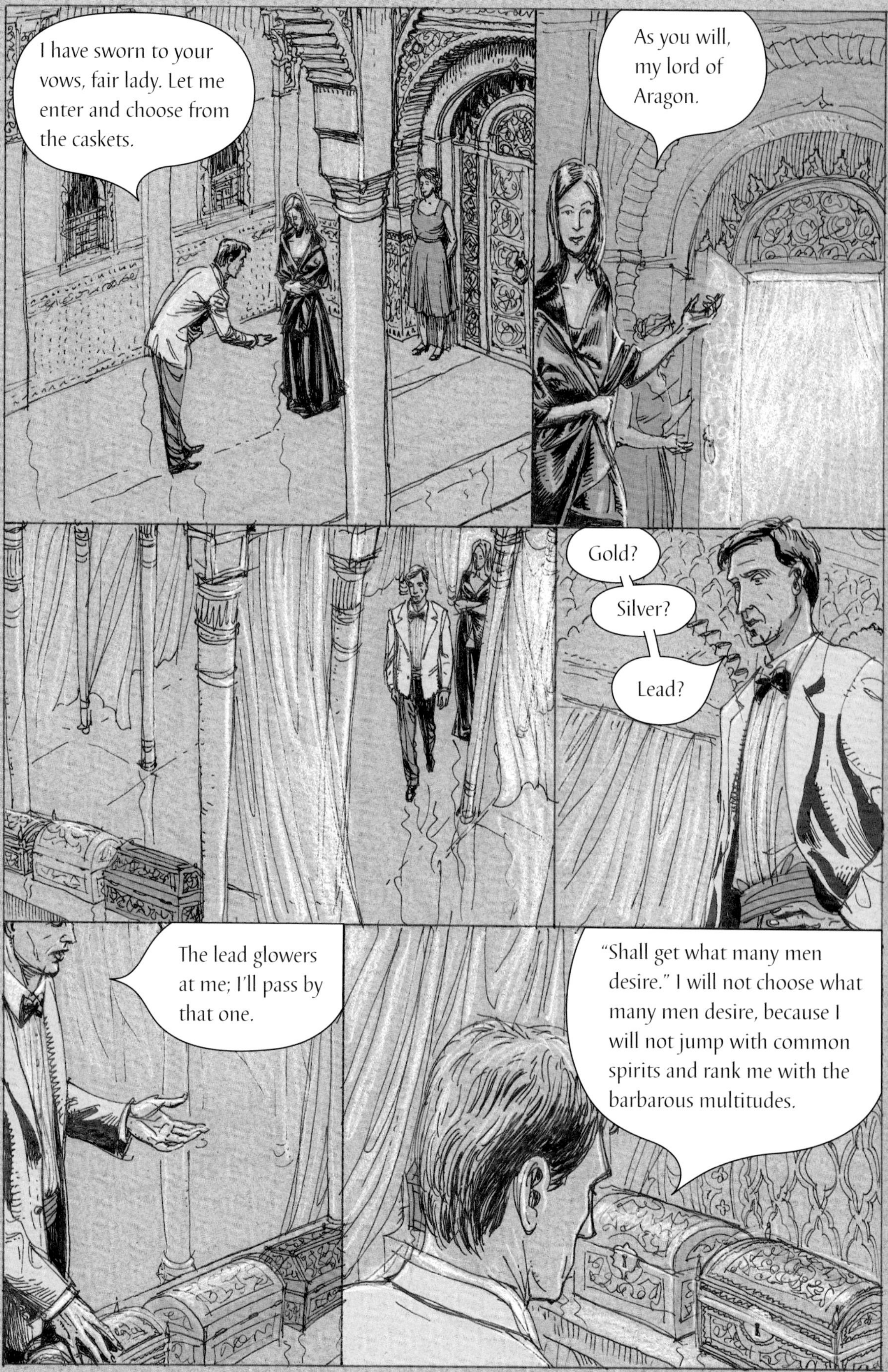
I have sworn to your vows, fair lady. Let me enter and choose from the caskets.
As you will, my lord of Aragon.
Gold?
Silver?
Lead?
The lead glowers at me; I'll pass by that one.
"Shall get what many men desire." I will not choose what many men desire, because I will not jump with common spirits and rank me with the barbarous multitudes.

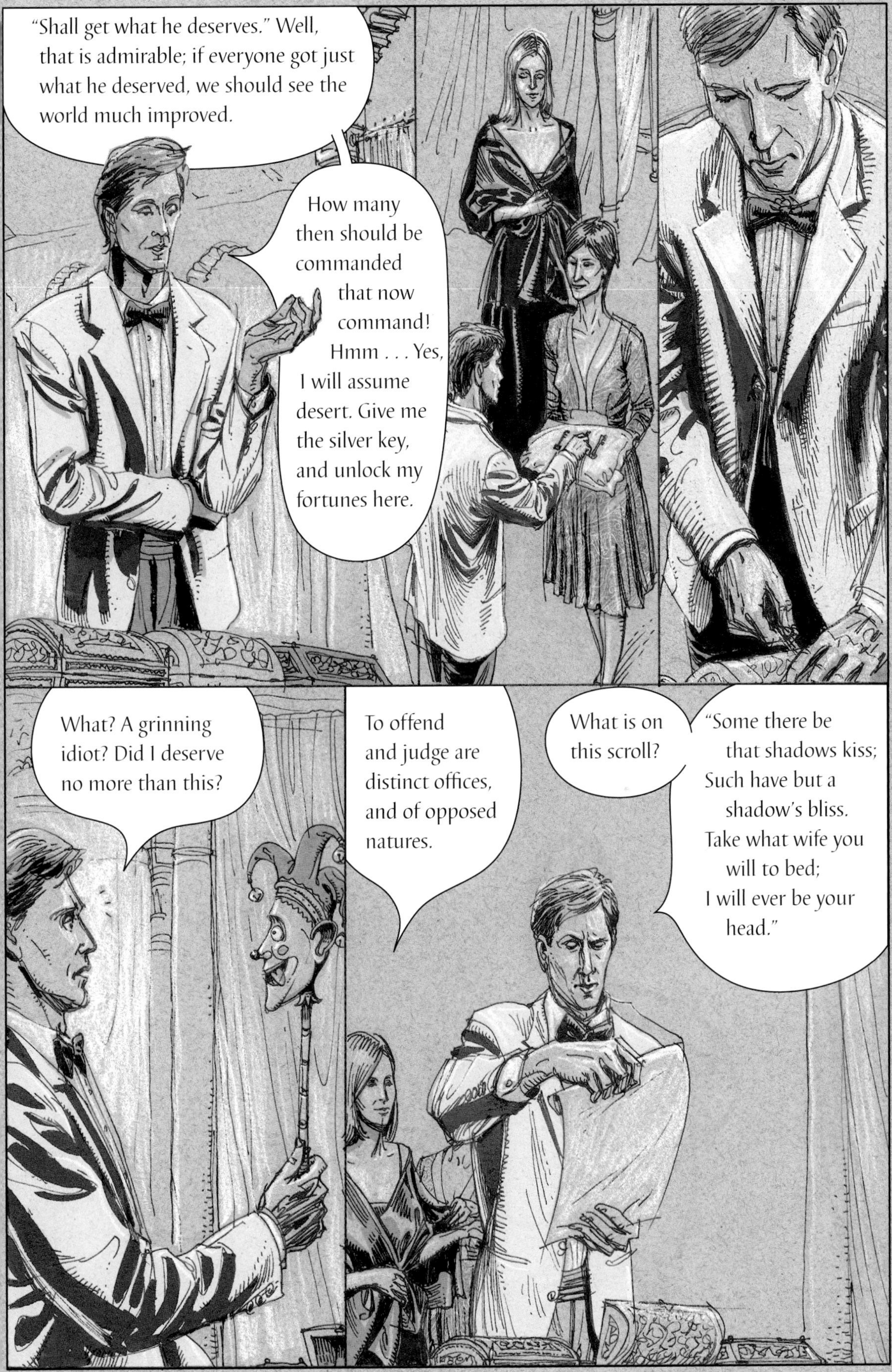
"Shall get what he deserves." Well, that is admirable; if everyone got just what he deserved, we should see the world much improved.
How many then should be commanded that now command! Hmm . . . Yes, I will assume desert. Give me the silver key, and unlock my fortunes here.
What? A grinning idiot? Did I deserve no more than this?
To offend and judge are distinct offices, and of opposed natures.
What is on this scroll?
"Some there be that shadows kiss; Such have but a shadow's bliss. Take what wife you will to bed; I will ever be your head."

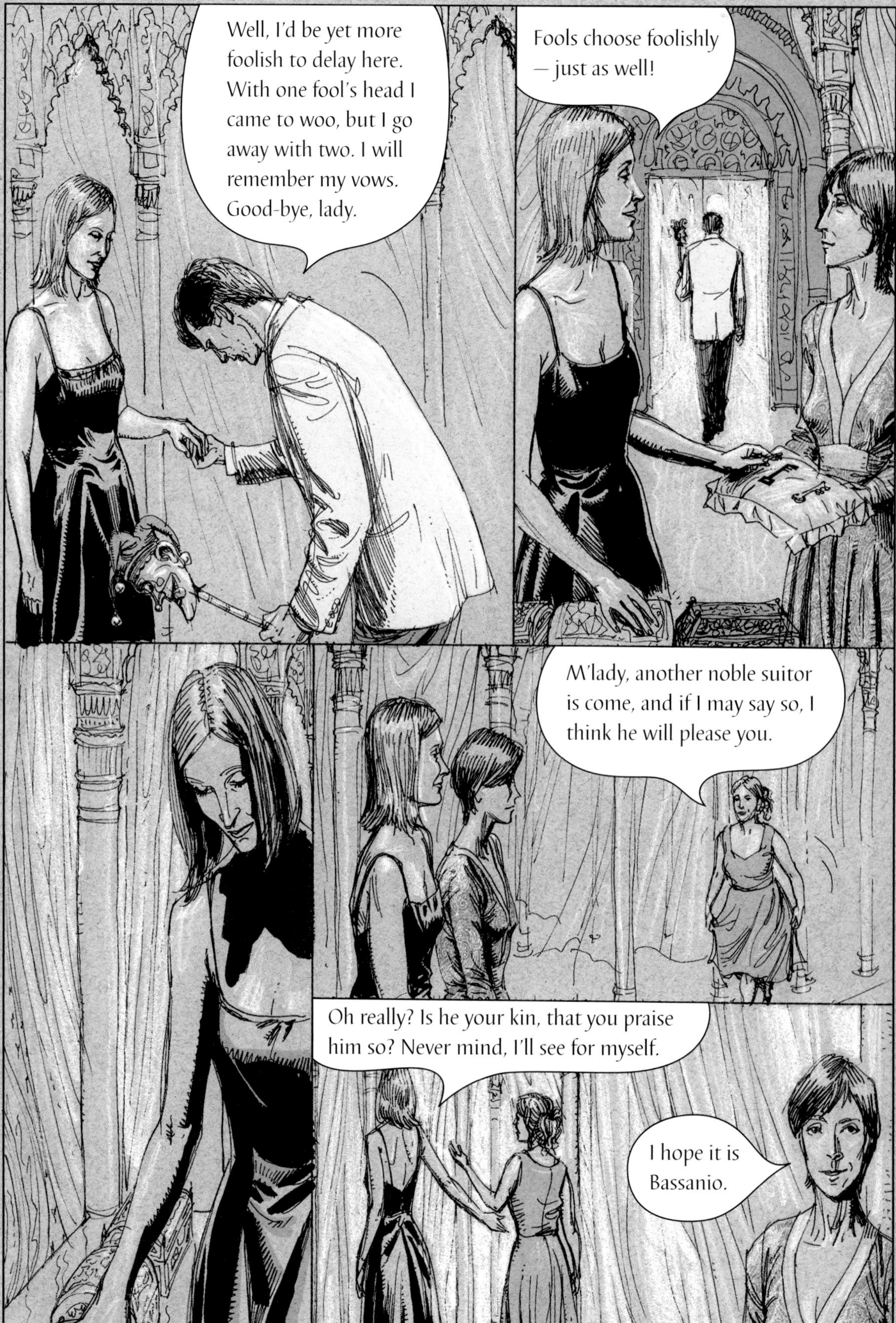
Well, I'd be yet more foolish to delay here. With one fool's head I came to woo, but I go away with two. I will remember my vows. Good-bye, lady.
Fools choose foolishly — just as well!
M'lady, another noble suitor is come, and if I may say so, I think he will please you.
Oh really? Is he your kin, that you praise him so? Never mind, I'll see for myself.
I hope it is Bassanio.

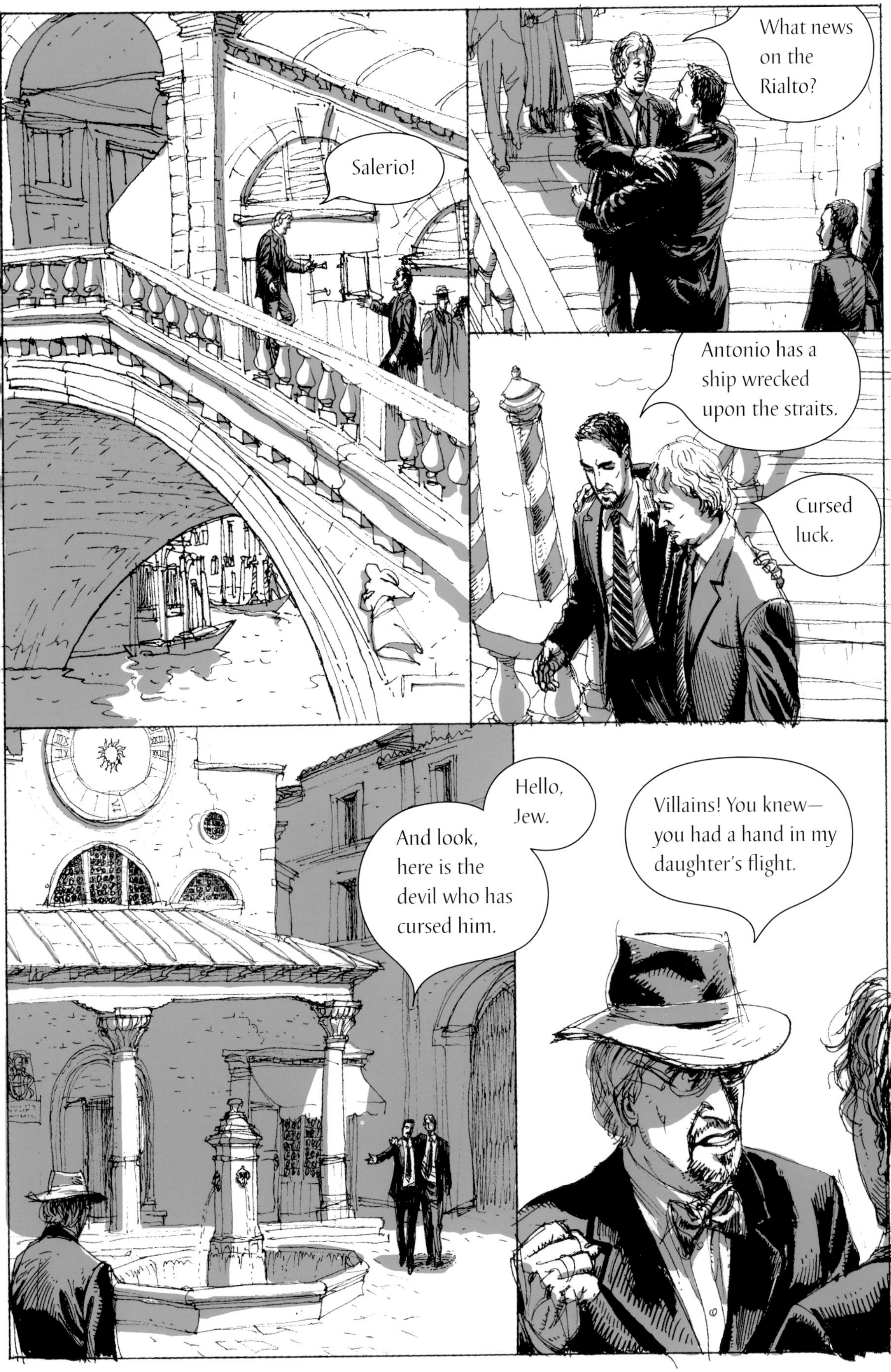
Salerio!
What news on the Rialto?
Antonio has a ship wrecked upon the straits.
Cursed luck.
Hello, Jew.
And look, here is the devil who has cursed him.
Villains! You knew— you had a hand in my daughter's flight.

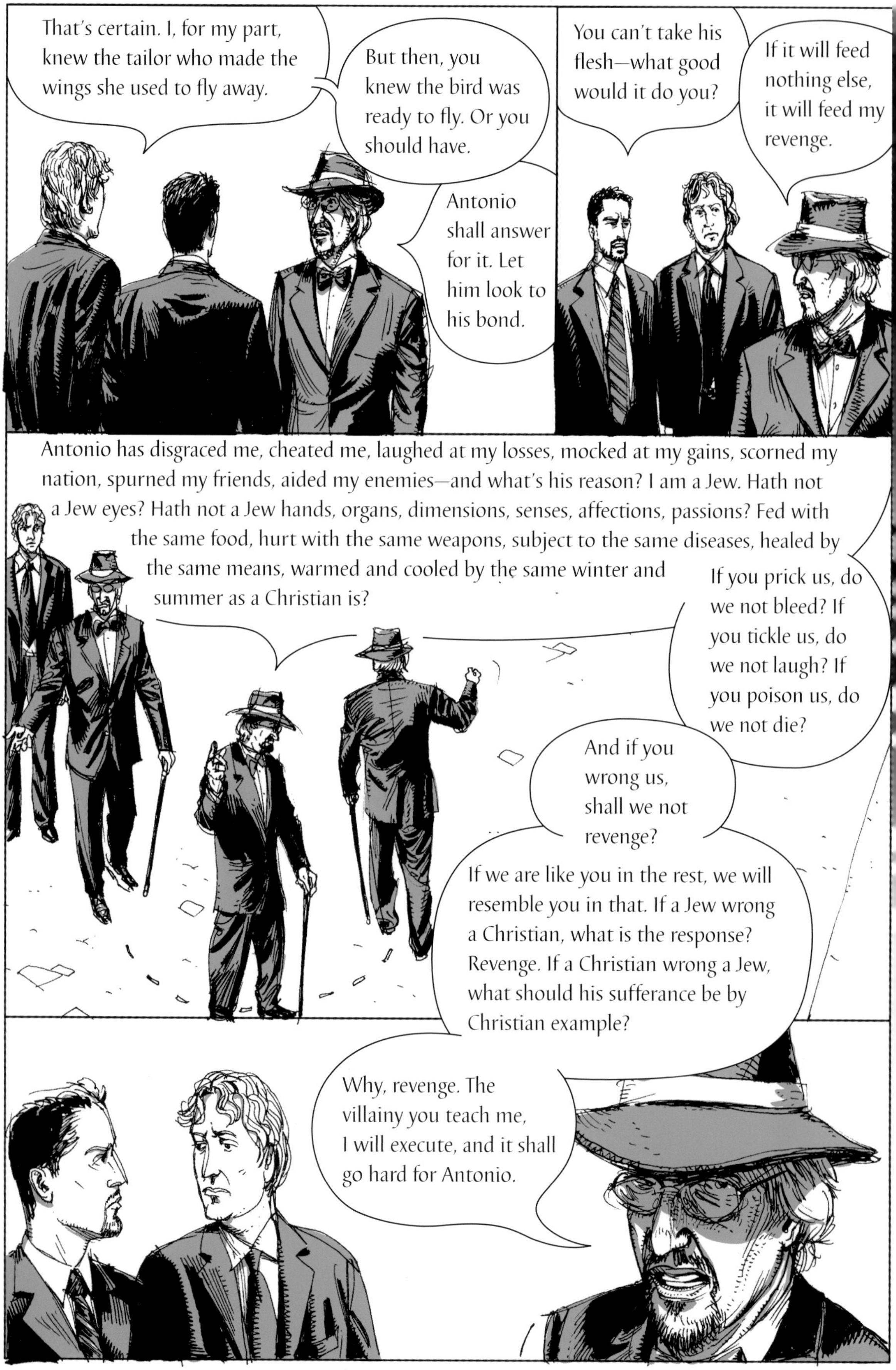
That's certain. I, for my part, knew the tailor who made the wings she used to fly away.
But then, you knew the bird was ready to fly. Or you should have.
Antonio shall answer for it. Let him look to his bond.
You can't take his flesh—what good would it do you?
If it will feed nothing else, it will feed my revenge.
Antonio has disgraced me, cheated me, laughed at my losses, mocked at my gains, scorned my nation, spurned my friends, aided my enemies—and what's his reason? I am a Jew. Hath not a Jew eyes? Hath not a Jew hands, organs, dimensions, senses, affections, passions? Fed with the same food, hurt with the same weapons, subject to the same diseases, healed by the same means, warmed and cooled by the same winter and summer as a Christian is?
If you prick us, do we not bleed? If you tickle us, do we not laugh? If you poison us, do we not die?
And if you wrong us, shall we not revenge?
If we are like you in the rest, we will resemble you in that. If a Jew wrong a Christian, what is the response? Revenge. If a Christian wrong a Jew, what should his sufferance be by Christian example?
Why, revenge. The villainy you teach me, I will execute, and it shall go hard for Antonio.

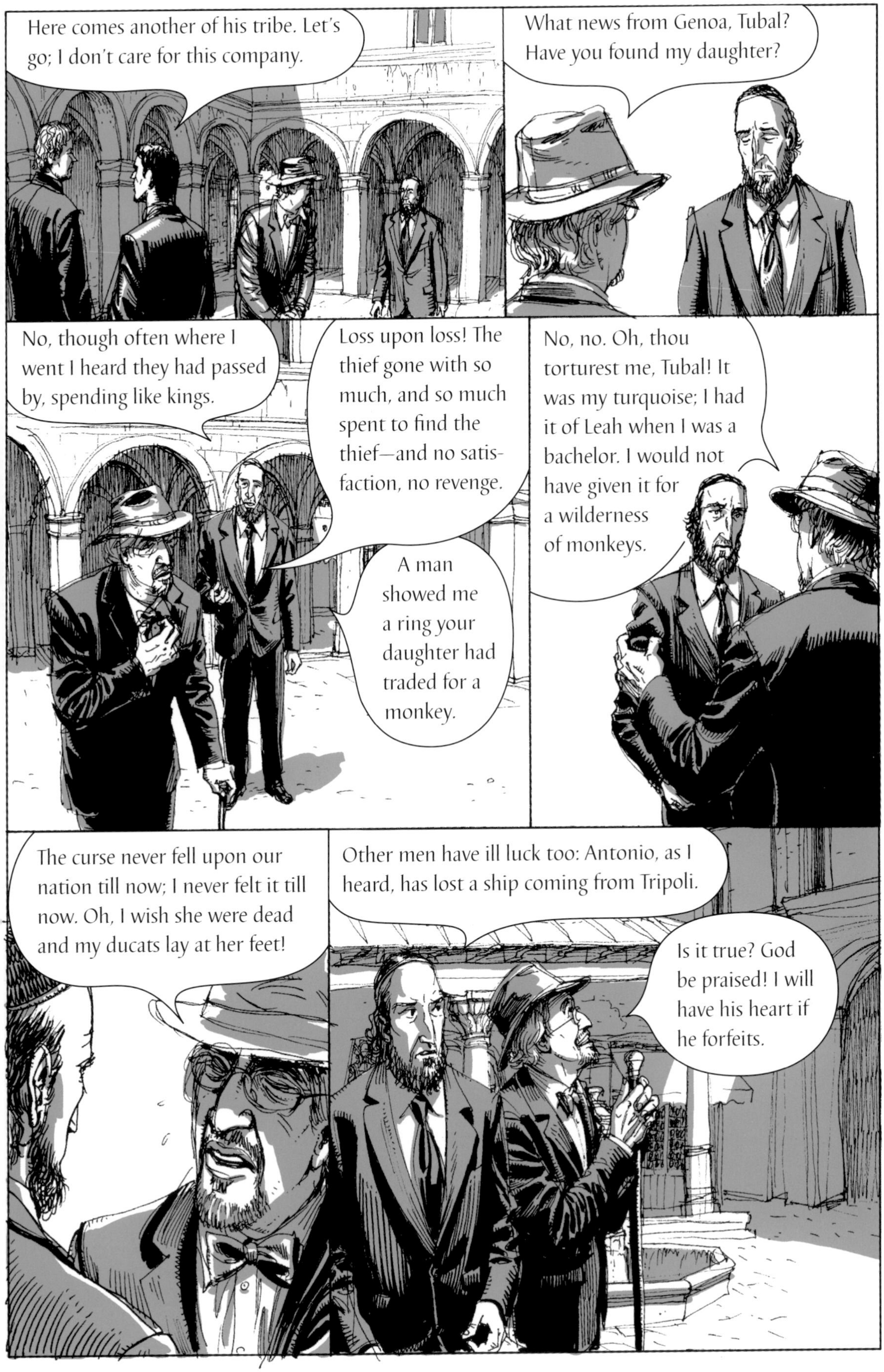
Here comes another of his tribe. Let's go; I don't care for this company.
What news from Genoa, Tubal? Have you found my daughter?
No, though often where I went I heard they had passed by, spending like kings.
Loss upon loss! The thief gone with so much, and so much spent to find the thief—and no satisfaction, no revenge.
A man showed me a ring your daughter had traded for a monkey.
No, no. Oh, thou torturest me, Tubal! It was my turquoise; I had it of Leah when I was a bachelor. I would not have given it for a wilderness of monkeys.
The curse never fell upon our nation till now; I never felt it till now. Oh, I wish she were dead and my ducats lay at her feet!
Other men have ill luck too: Antonio, as I heard, has lost a ship coming from Tripoli.
Is it true? God be praised! I will have his heart if he forfeits.

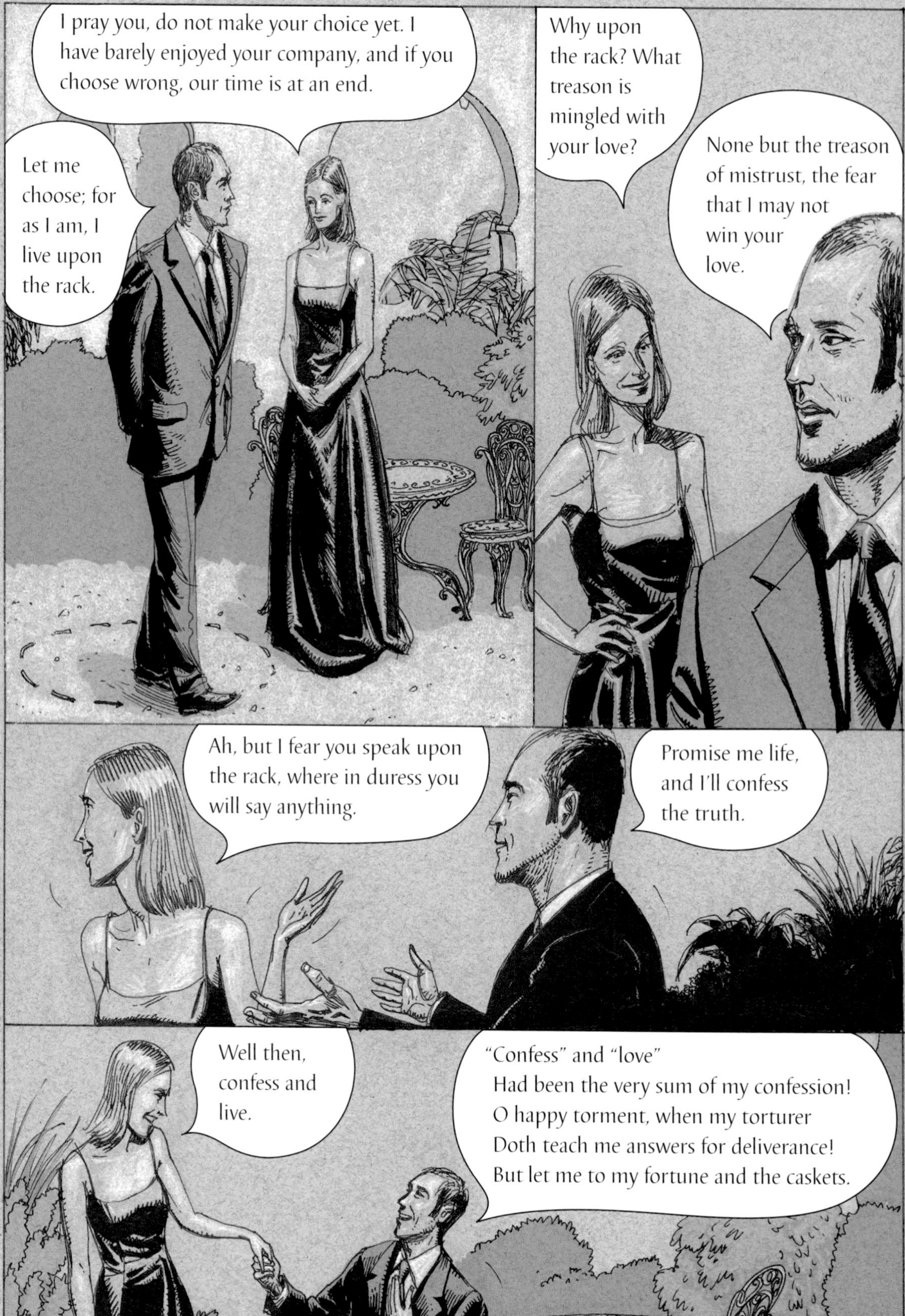
I pray you, do not make your choice yet. I have barely enjoyed your company, and if you choose wrong, our time is at an end.
Let me choose; for as I am, I live upon the rack.
Why upon the rack? What treason is mingled with your love?
None but the treason of mistrust, the fear that I may not win your love.
Ah, but I fear you speak upon the rack, where in duress you will say anything.
Promise me life, and I'll confess the truth.
Well then, confess and live.
"Confess" and "love"
Had been the very sum of my confession!
O happy torment, when my torturer
Doth teach me answers for deliverance!
But let me to my fortune and the caskets.

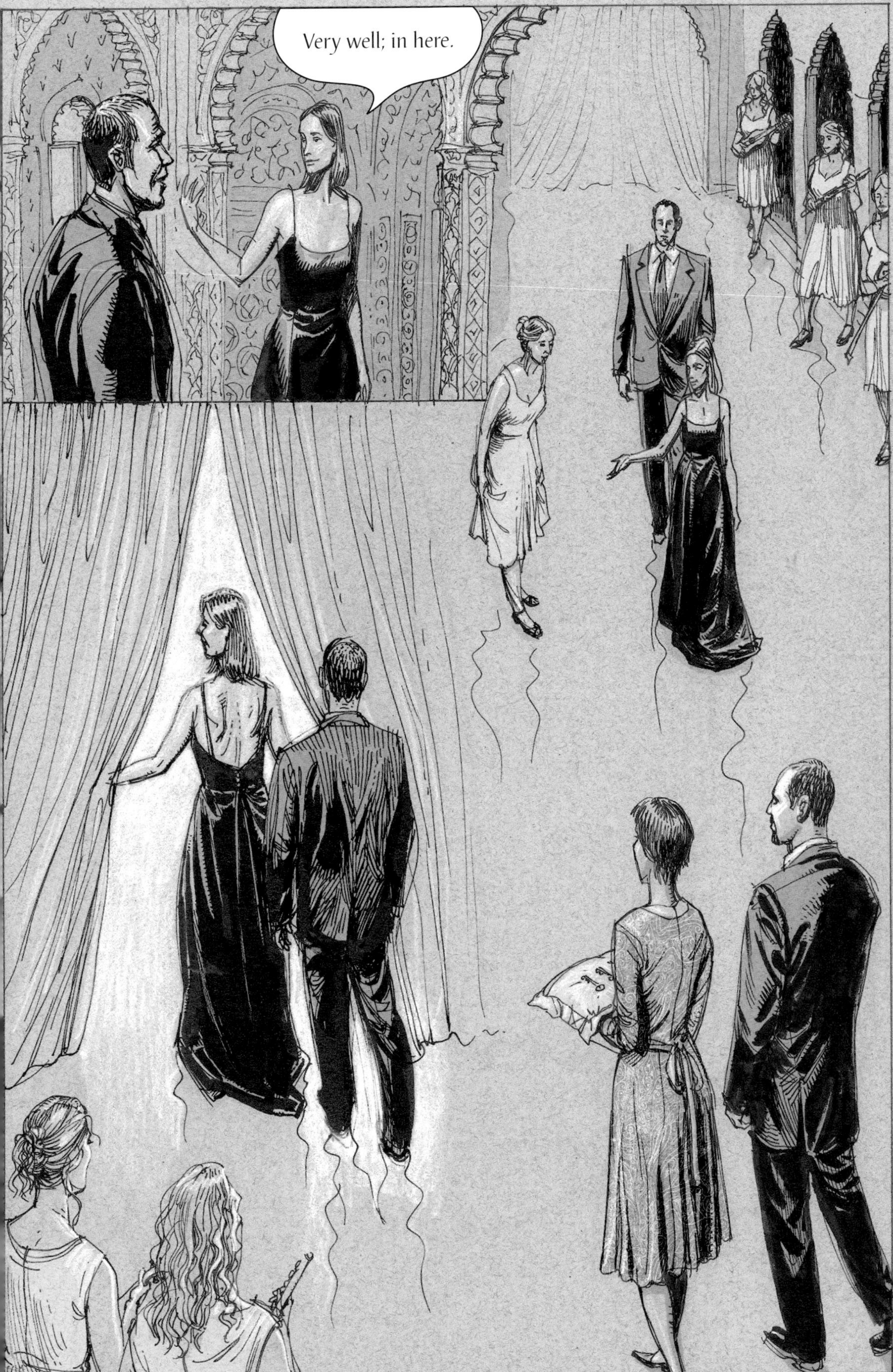
Very well; in here.

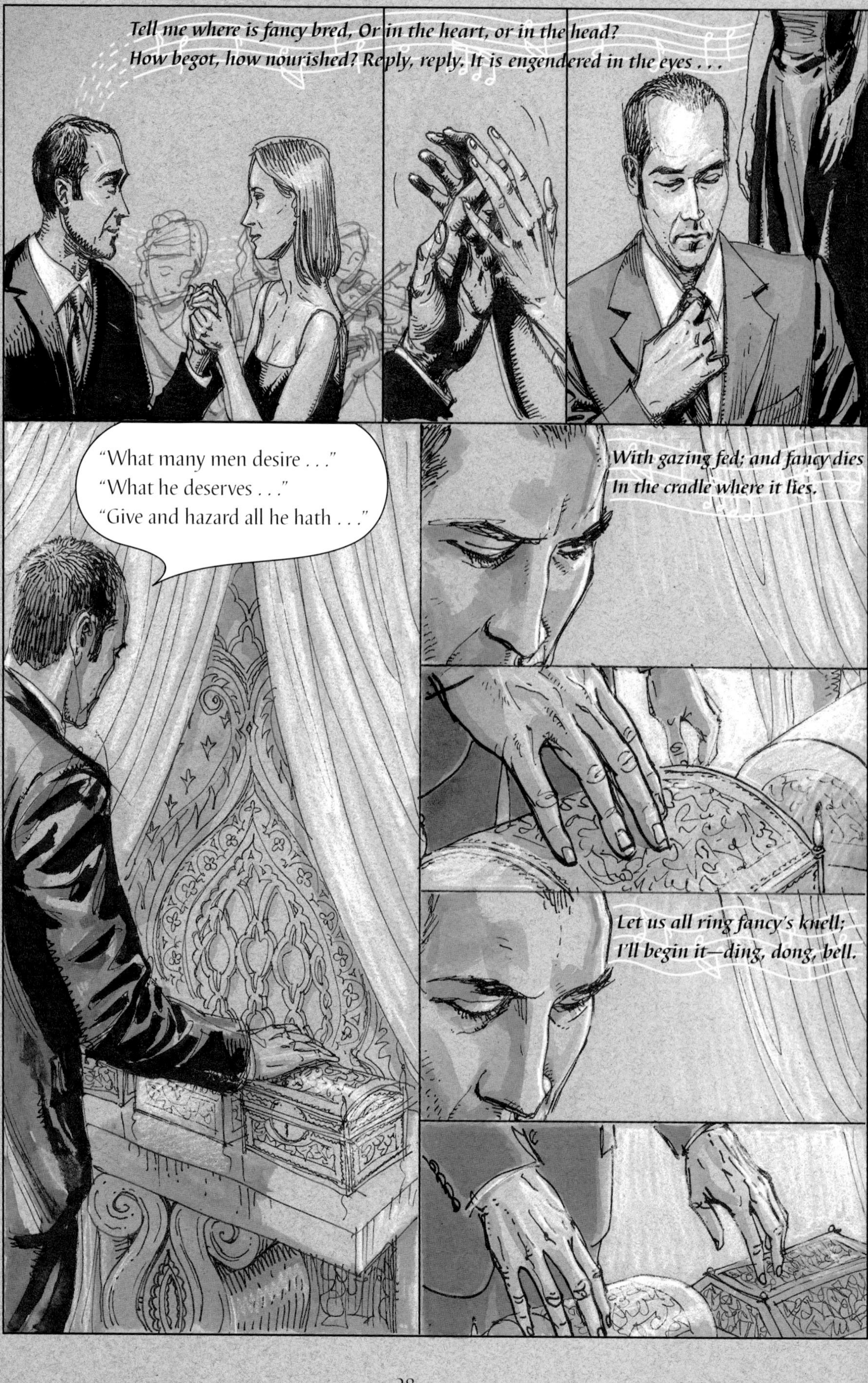

Tell me where is fancy bred, Or in the heart, or in the head?
How begot, how nourished? Reply, reply. It is engendered in the eyes . . .
"What many men desire . . ."
"What he deserves . . ."
"Give and hazard all he hath . . ."
With gazing fed; and fancy dies
In the cradle where it lies.
Let us all ring fancy's knell;
I'll begin it—ding, dong, bell.

33

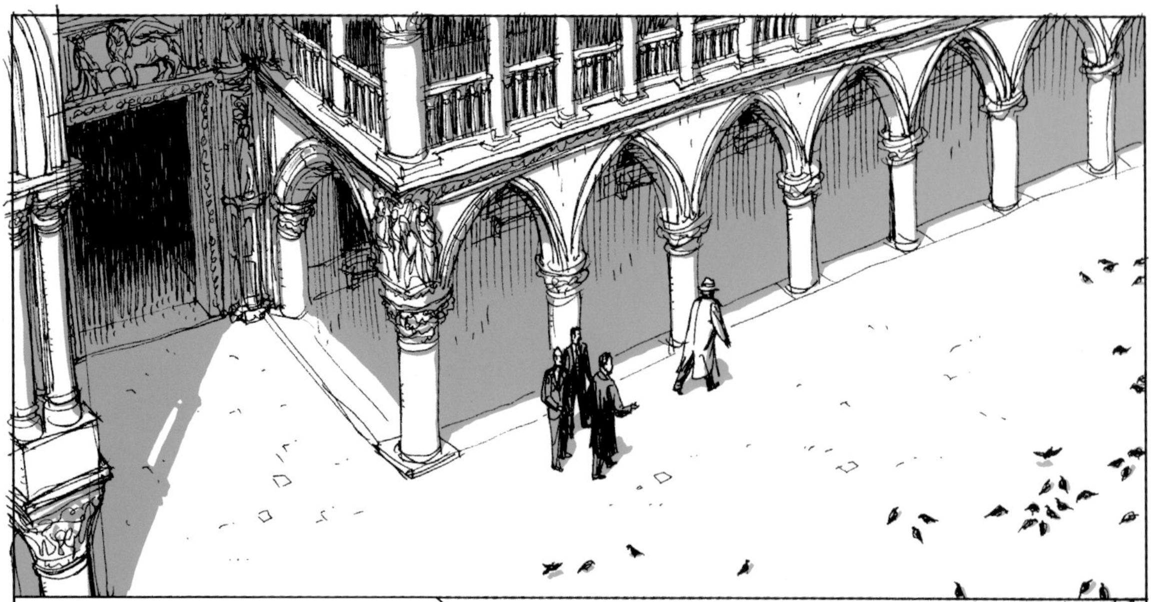

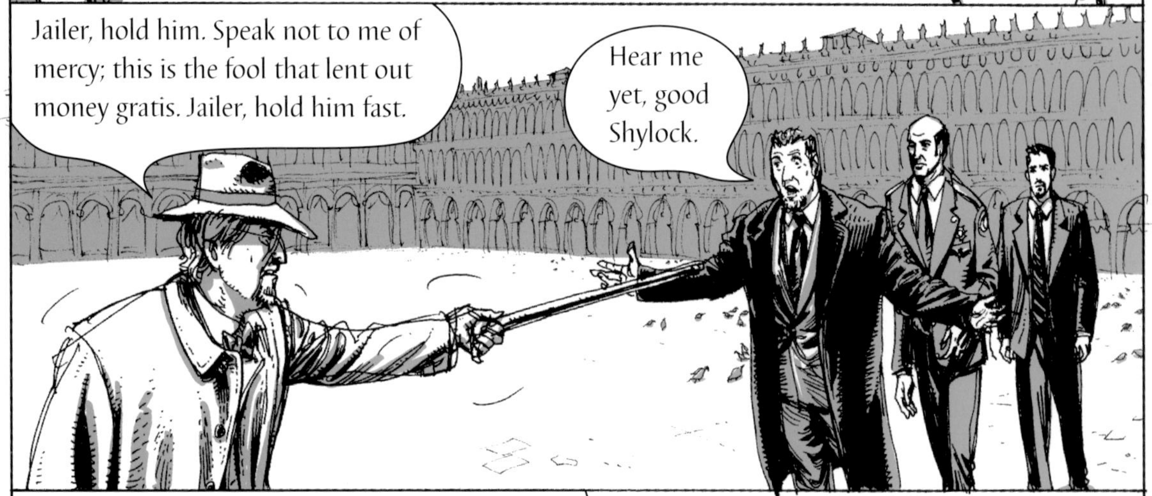
Jailer, hold him. Speak not to me of mercy; this is the fool that lent out money gratis. Jailer, hold him fast.
Hear me yet, good Shylock.

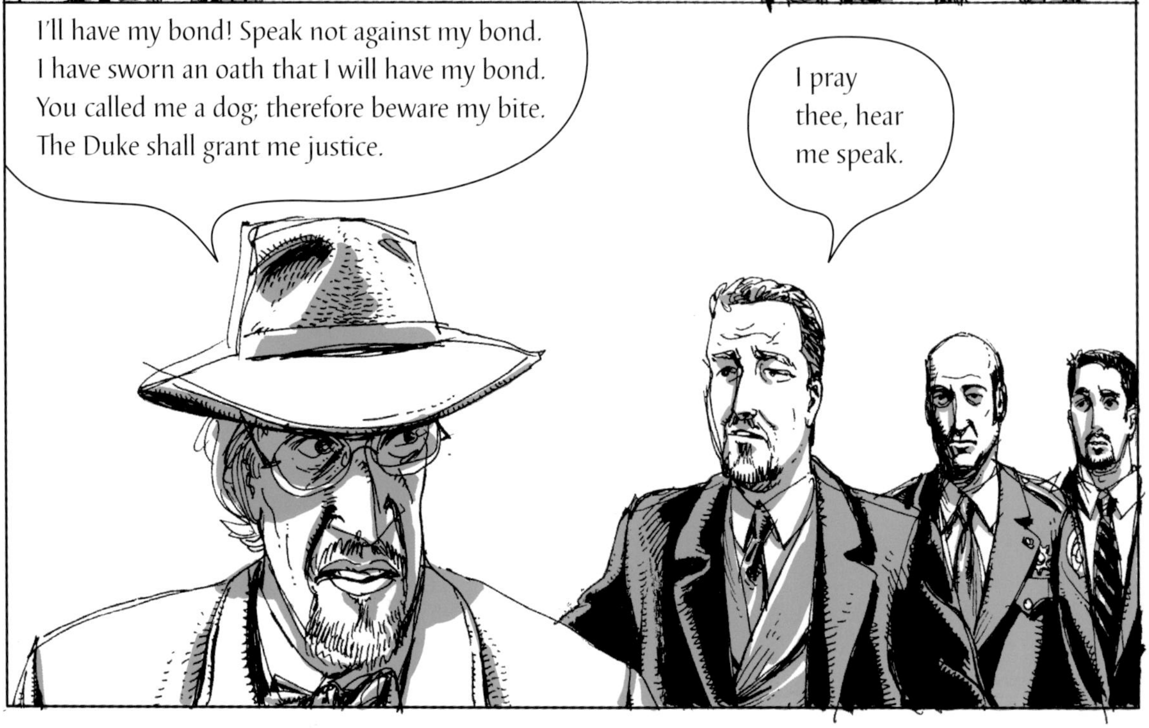
I'll have my bond! Speak not against my bond. I have sworn an oath that I will have my bond. You called me a dog; therefore beware my bite. The Duke shall grant me justice.
I pray thee, hear me speak.

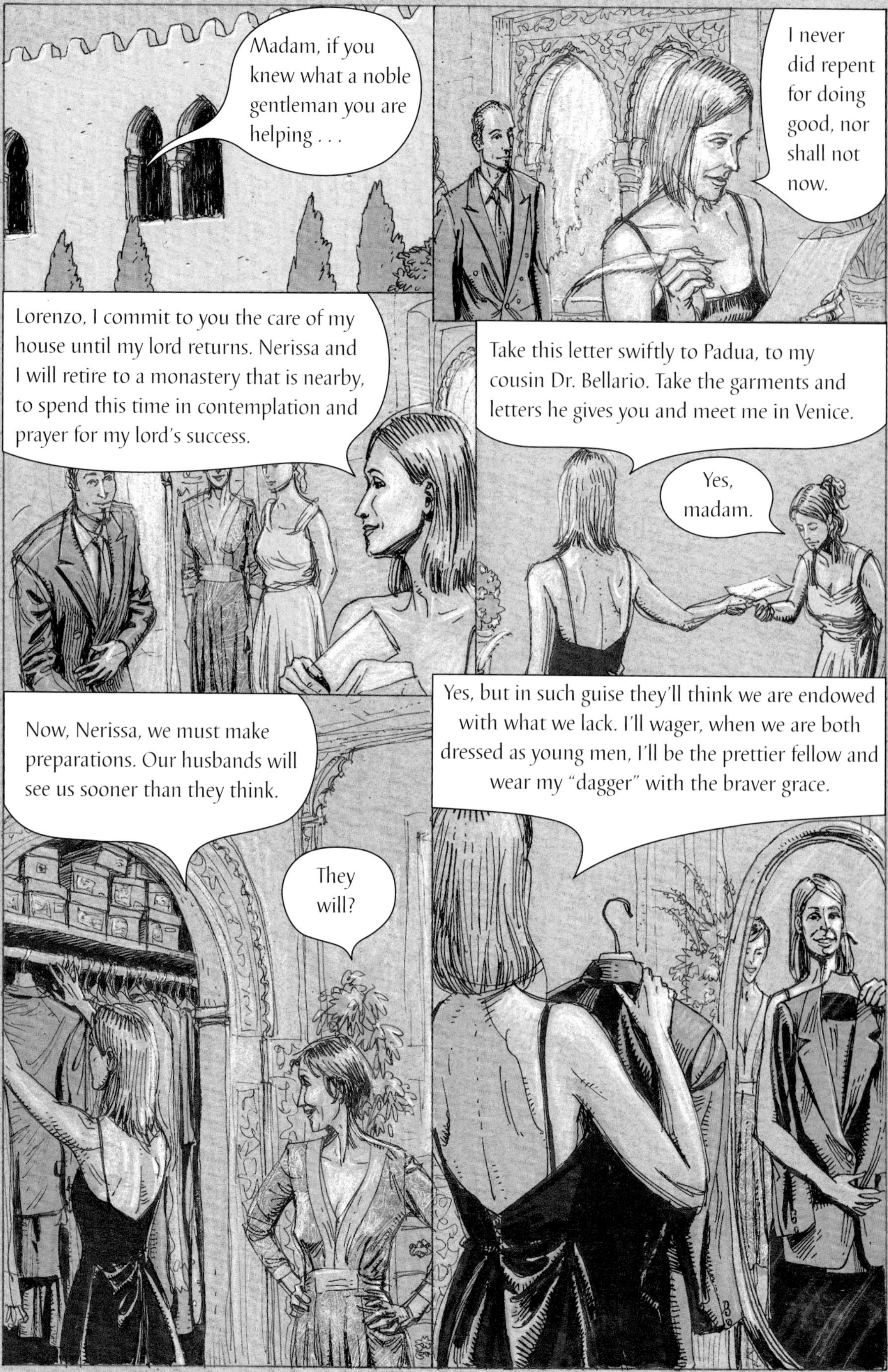
Madam, if you knew what a noble gentleman you are helping . . .
I never did repent for doing good, nor shall not now.
Lorenzo, I commit to you the care of my house until my lord returns. Nerissa and I will retire to a monastery that is nearby, to spend this time in contemplation and prayer for my lord's success.
Take this letter swiftly to Padua, to my cousin Dr. Bellario. Take the garments and letters he gives you and meet me in Venice.
Yes, madam.
Now, Nerissa, we must make preparations. Our husbands will see us sooner than they think.
They will?
Yes, but in such guise they'll think we are endowed with what we lack. I'll wager, when we are both dressed as young men, I'll be the prettier fellow and wear my "dagger" with the braver grace.

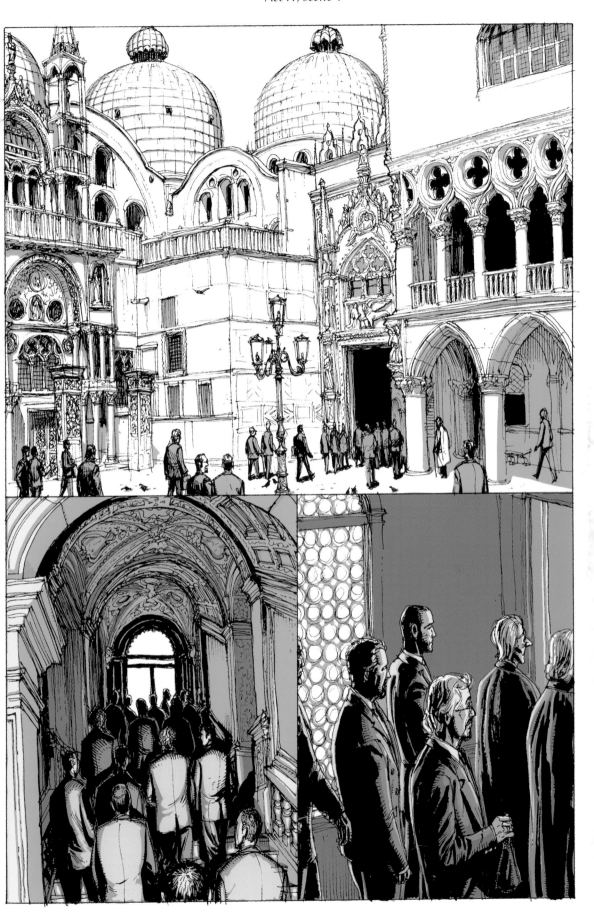

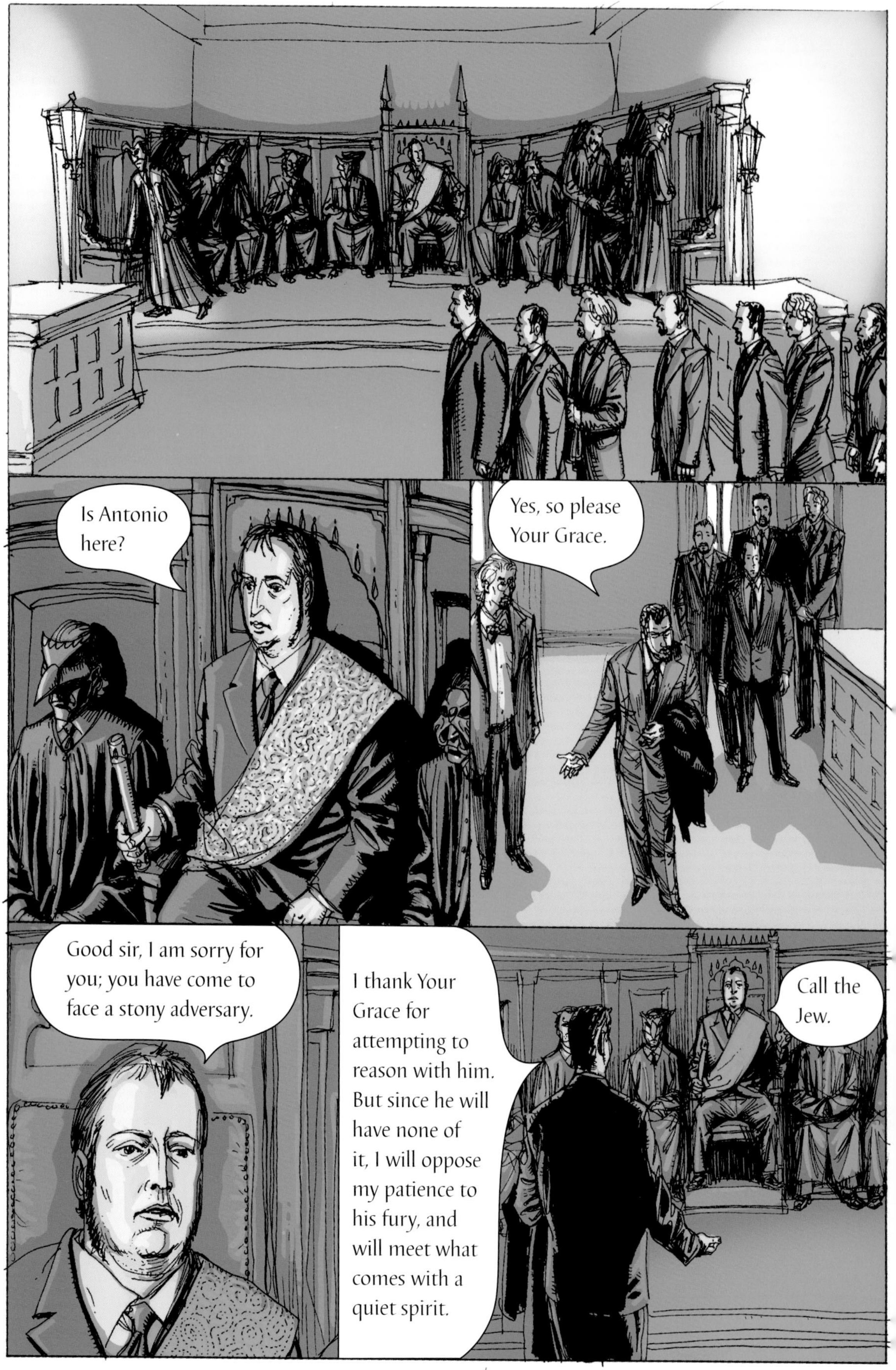

Is Antonio here?
Yes, so please Your Grace.
Good sir, I am sorry for you; you have come to face a stony adversary.
I thank Your Grace for attempting to reason with him. But since he will have none of it, I will oppose my patience to his fury, and will meet what comes with a quiet spirit.
Call the Jew.

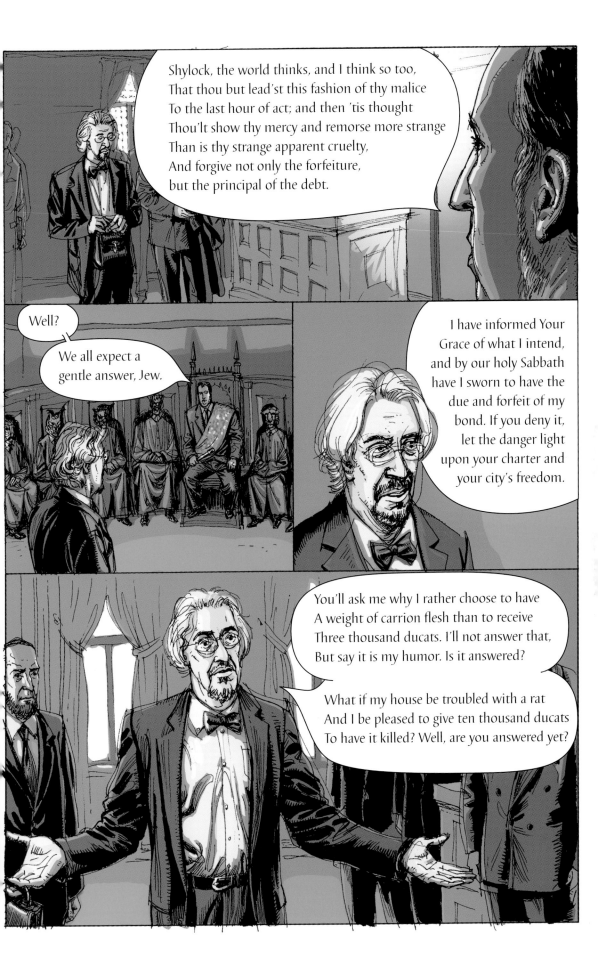

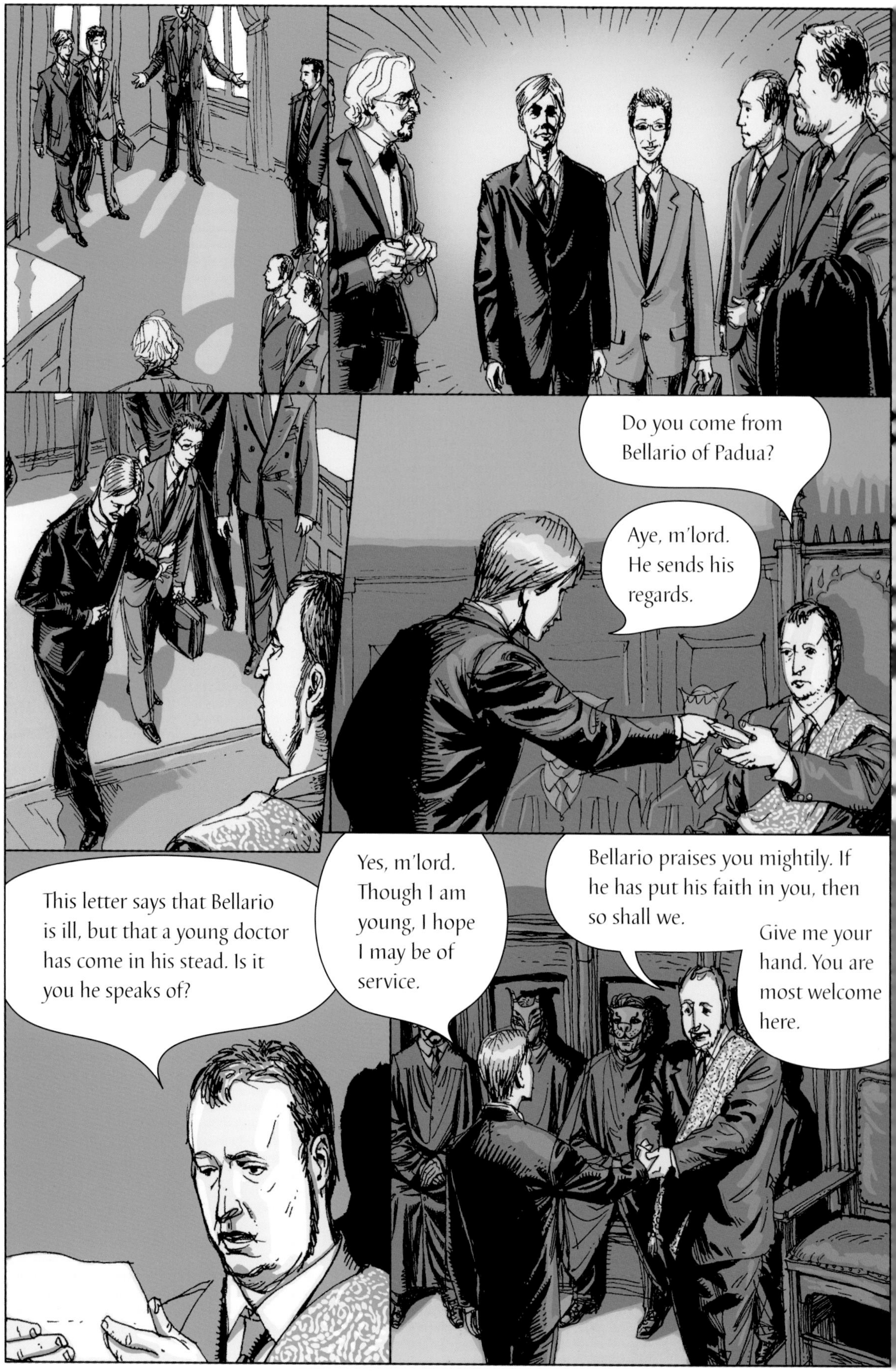

Do you come from Bellario of Padua?
Aye, m'lord. He sends his regards.
This letter says that Bellario is ill, but that a young doctor has come in his stead. Is it you he speaks of?
Yes, m'lord. Though I am young, I hope I may be of service.
Bellario praises you mightily. If he has put his faith in you, then so shall we.
Give me your hand. You are most welcome here.

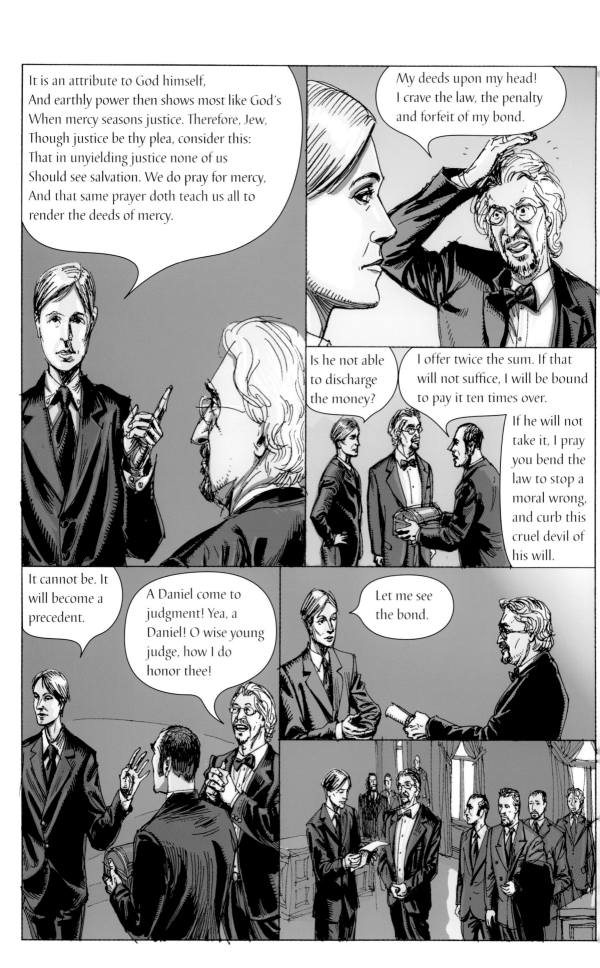

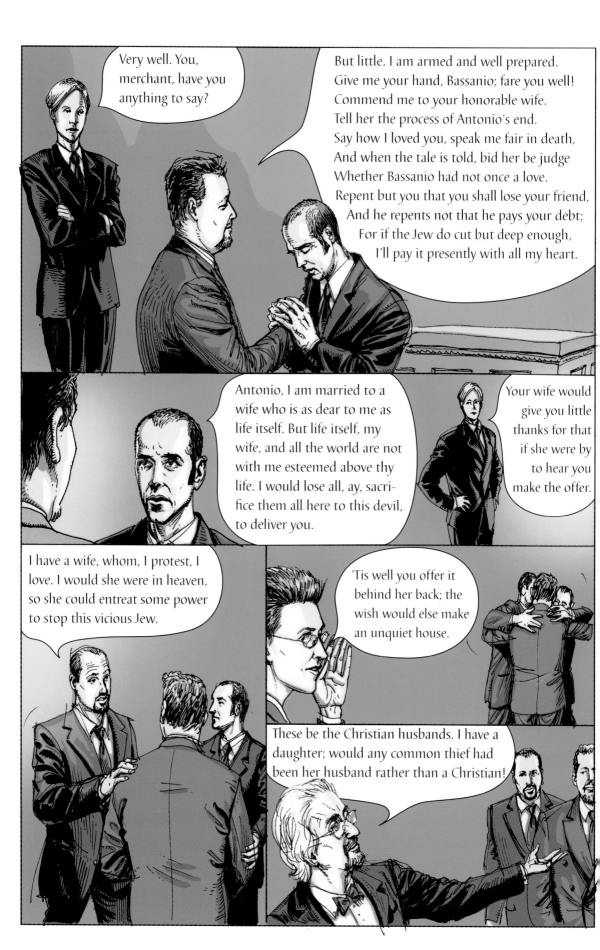

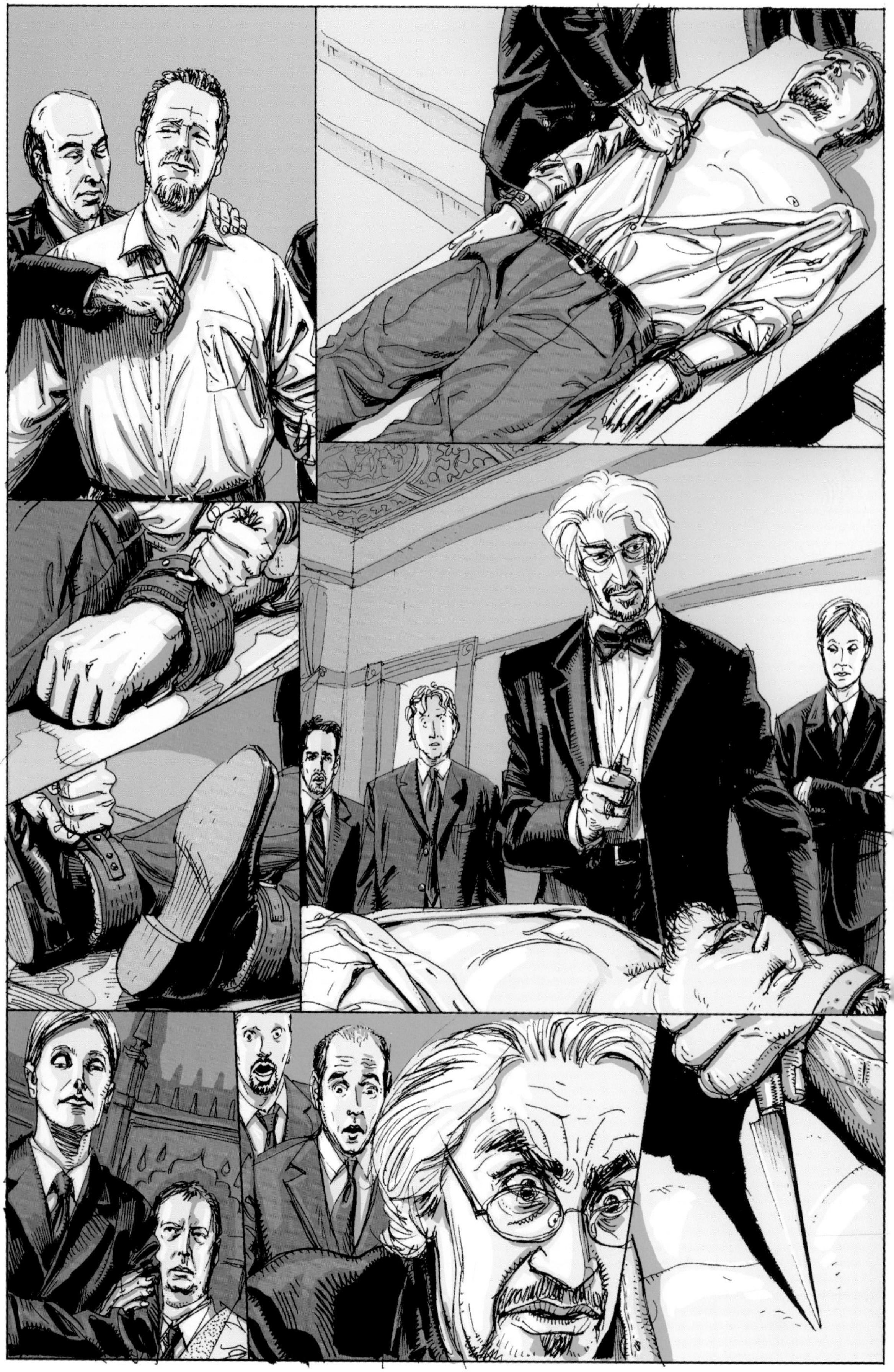

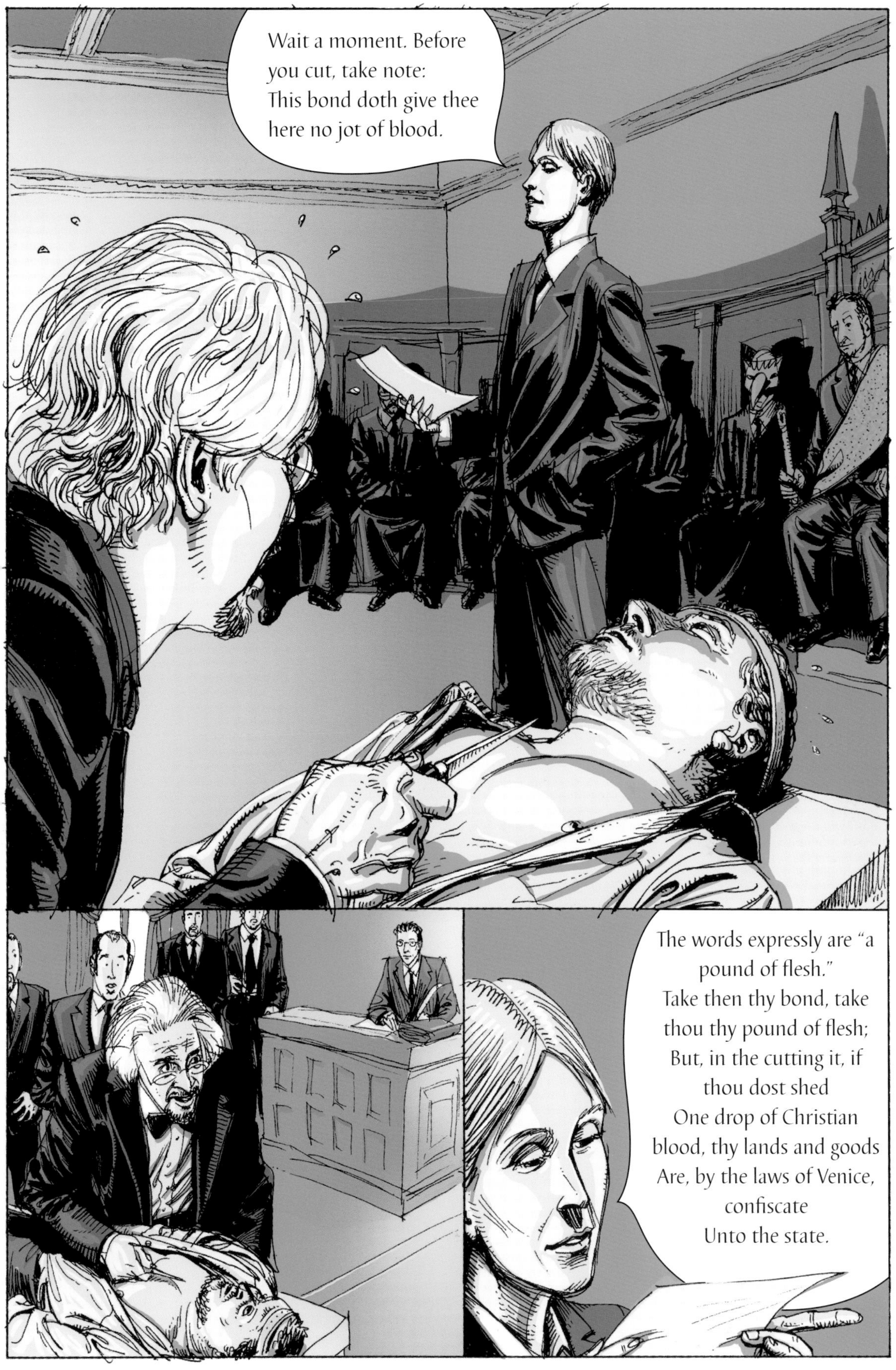
Wait a moment. Before you cut, take note:
This bond doth give thee here no jot of blood.
The words expressly are "a pound of flesh."
Take then thy bond, take thou thy pound of flesh;
But, in the cutting it, if thou dost shed
One drop of Christian blood, thy lands and goods
Are, by the laws of Venice, confiscate
Unto the state.

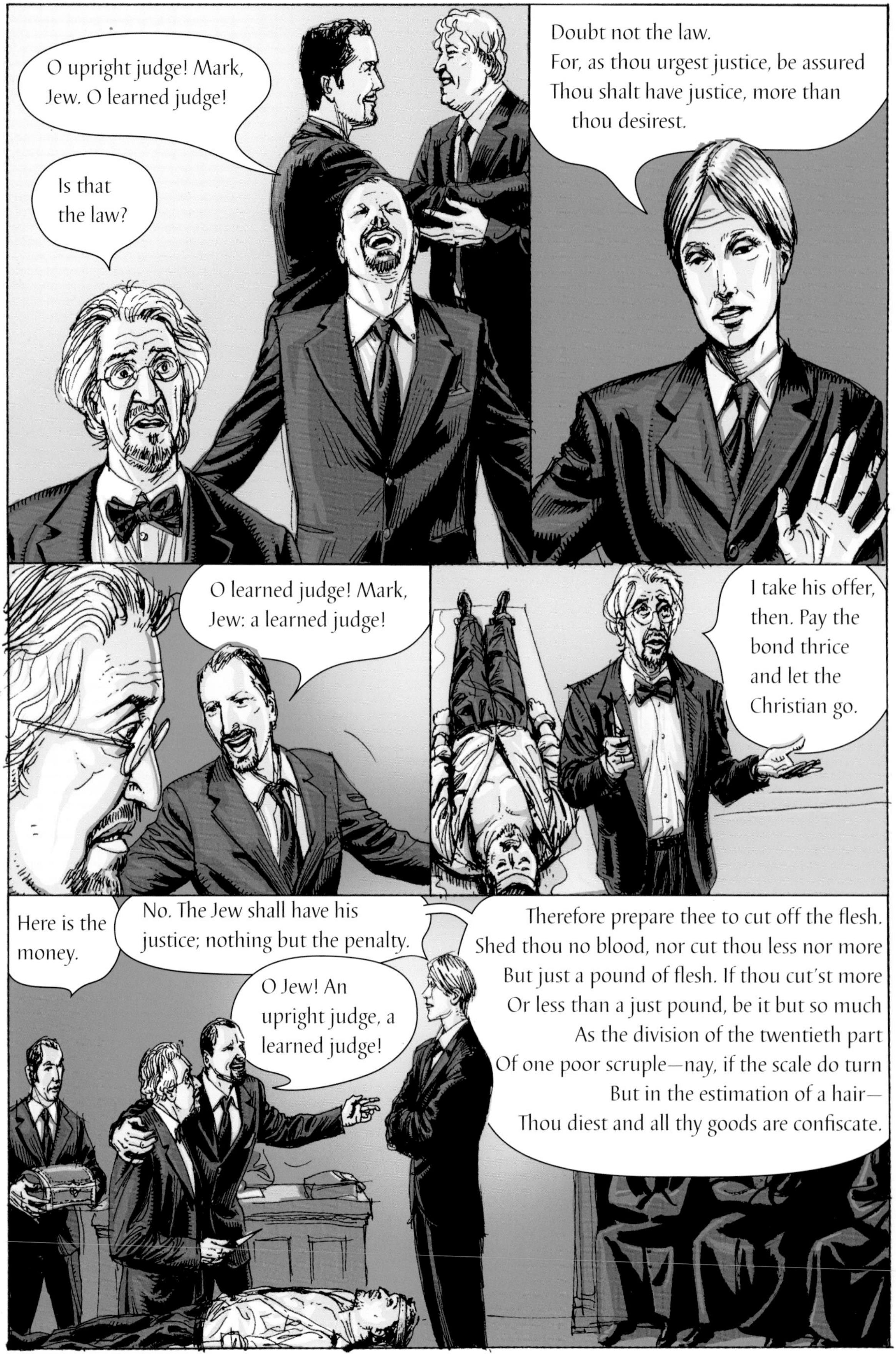
O upright judge! Mark, Jew. O learned judge!
Is that the law?
Doubt not the law.
For, as thou urgest justice, be assured
Thou shalt have justice, more than
thou desirest.
O learned judge! Mark, Jew: a learned judge!
I take his offer, then. Pay the bond thrice and let the Christian go.
Here is the money.
No. The Jew shall have his justice; nothing but the penalty.
O Jew! An upright judge, a learned judge!
Therefore prepare thee to cut off the flesh.
Shed thou no blood, nor cut thou less nor more
But just a pound of flesh. If thou cut'st more
Or less than a just pound, be it but so much
As the division of the twentieth part
Of one poor scruple—nay, if the scale do turn
But in the estimation of a hair—
Thou diest and all thy goods are confiscate.

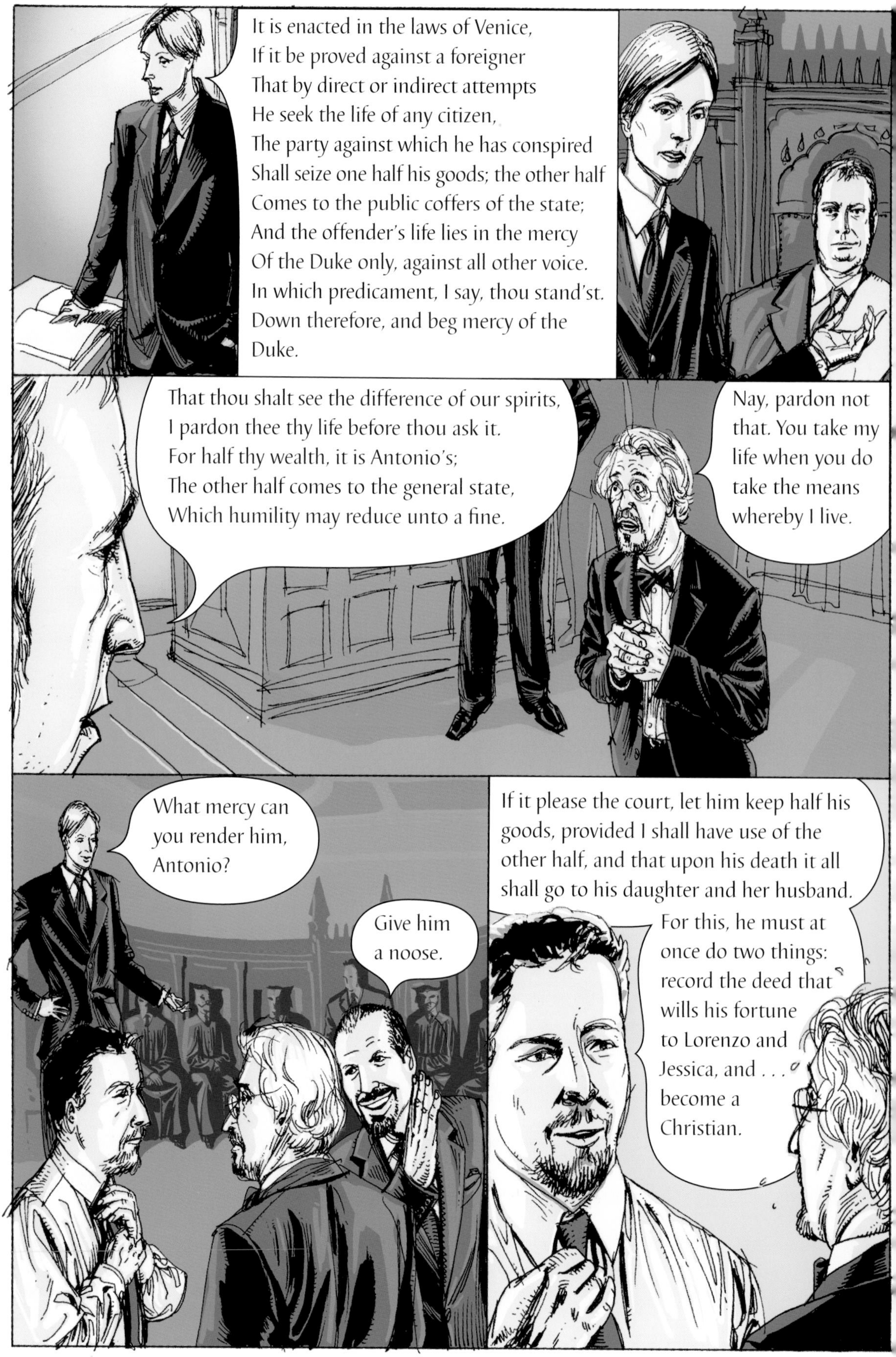
It is enacted in the laws of Venice,
If it be proved against a foreigner
That by direct or indirect attempts
He seek the life of any citizen,
The party against which he has conspired
Shall seize one half his goods; the other half
Comes to the public coffers of the state;
And the offender's life lies in the mercy
Of the Duke only, against all other voice.
In which predicament, I say, thou stand'st.
Down therefore, and beg mercy of the Duke.
That thou shalt see the difference of our spirits,
I pardon thee thy life before thou ask it.
For half thy wealth, it is Antonio's;
The other half comes to the general state,
Which humility may reduce unto a fine.
Nay, pardon not that. You take my life when you do take the means whereby I live.
What mercy can you render him, Antonio?
Give him a noose.
If it please the court, let him keep half his goods, provided I shall have use of the other half, and that upon his death it all shall go to his daughter and her husband.
For this, he must at once do two things: record the deed that wills his fortune to Lorenzo and Jessica, and . . . become a Christian.

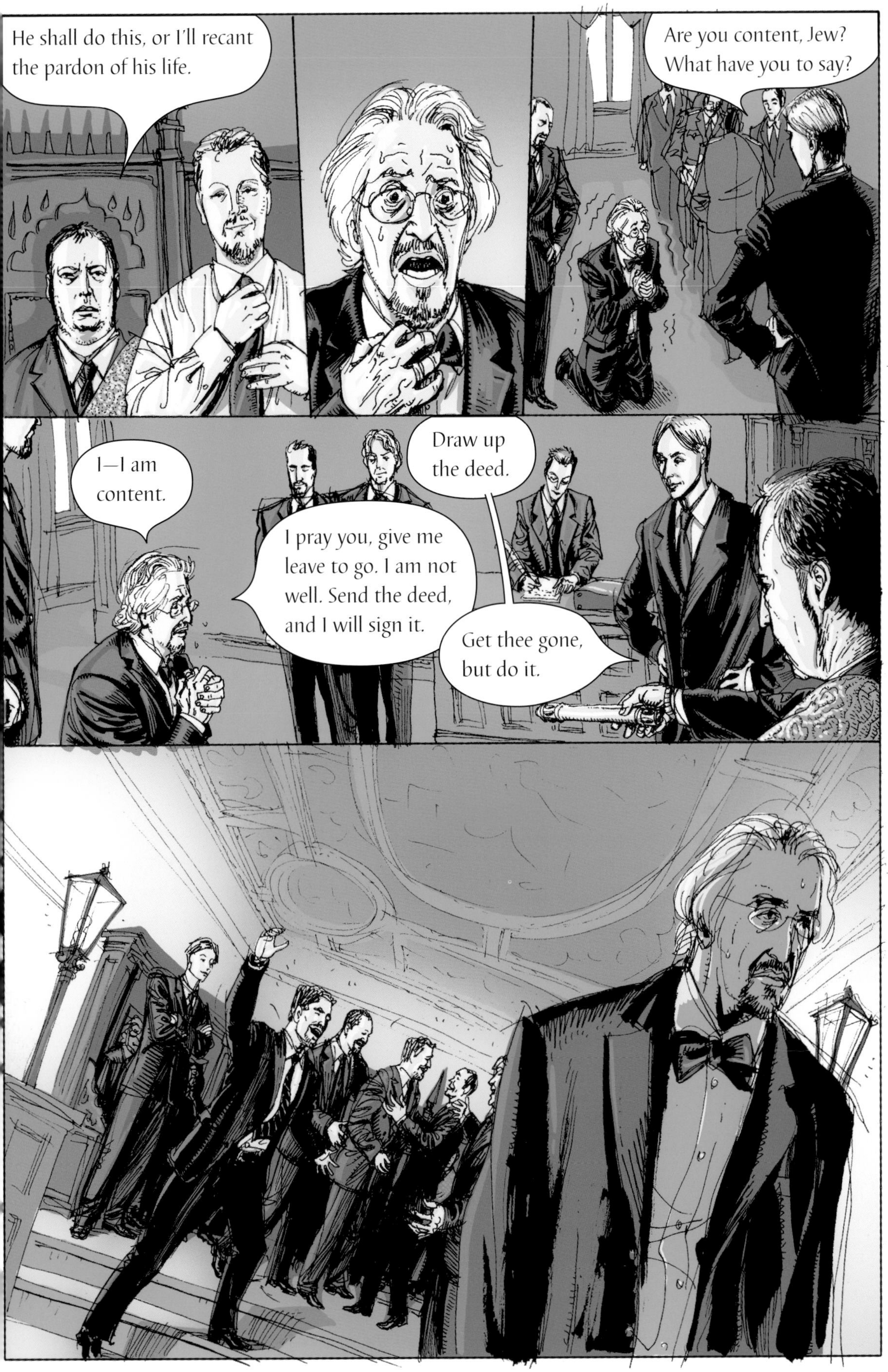
He shall do this, or I'll recant the pardon of his life.
Are you content, Jew? What have you to say?
I—I am content.
Draw up the deed.
I pray you, give me leave to go. I am not well. Send the deed, and I will sign it.
Get thee gone, but do it.

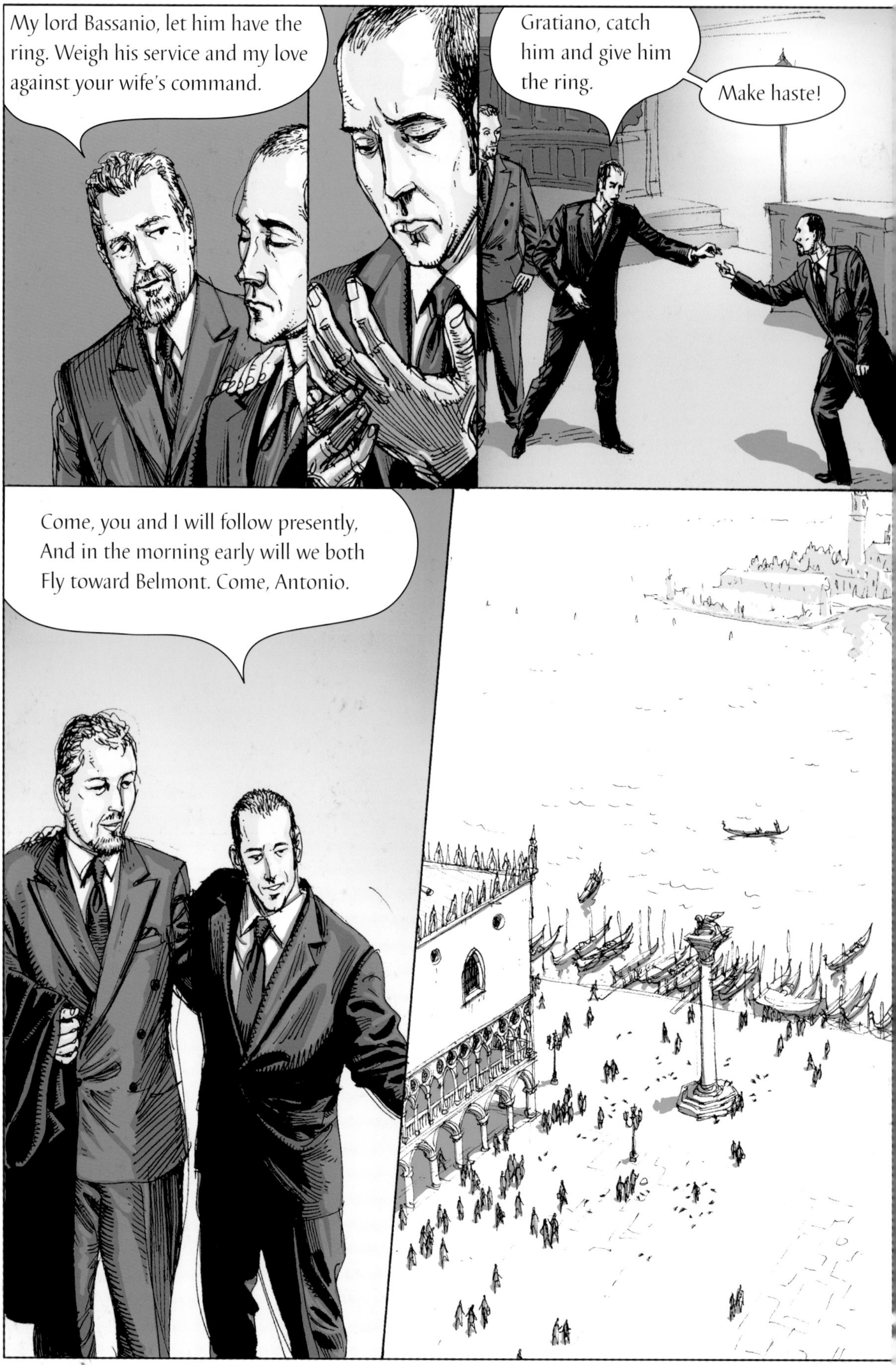
My lord Bassanio, let him have the ring. Weigh his service and my love against your wife's command.
Gratiano, catch him and give him the ring.
Make haste!
Come, you and I will follow presently,
And in the morning early will we both
Fly toward Belmont. Come, Antonio.

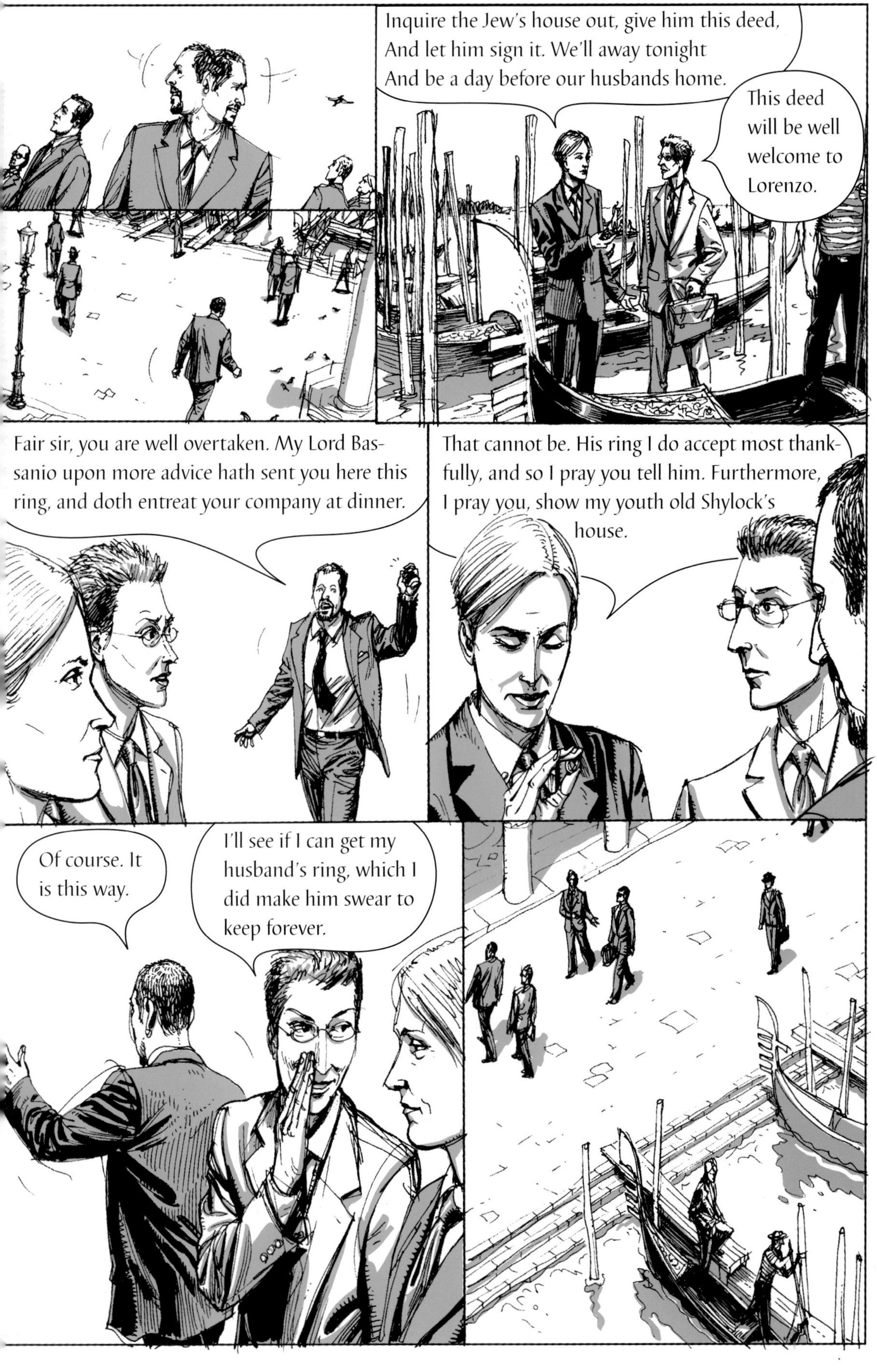
Inquire the Jew's house out, give him this deed,
And let him sign it. We'll away tonight
And be a day before our husbands home.
This deed will be well welcome to Lorenzo.
Fair sir, you are well overtaken. My Lord Bassanio upon more advice hath sent you here this ring, and doth entreat your company at dinner.
That cannot be. His ring I do accept most thankfully, and so I pray you tell him. Furthermore, I pray you, show my youth old Shylock's house.
Of course. It is this way.
I'll see if I can get my husband's ring, which I did make him swear to keep forever.

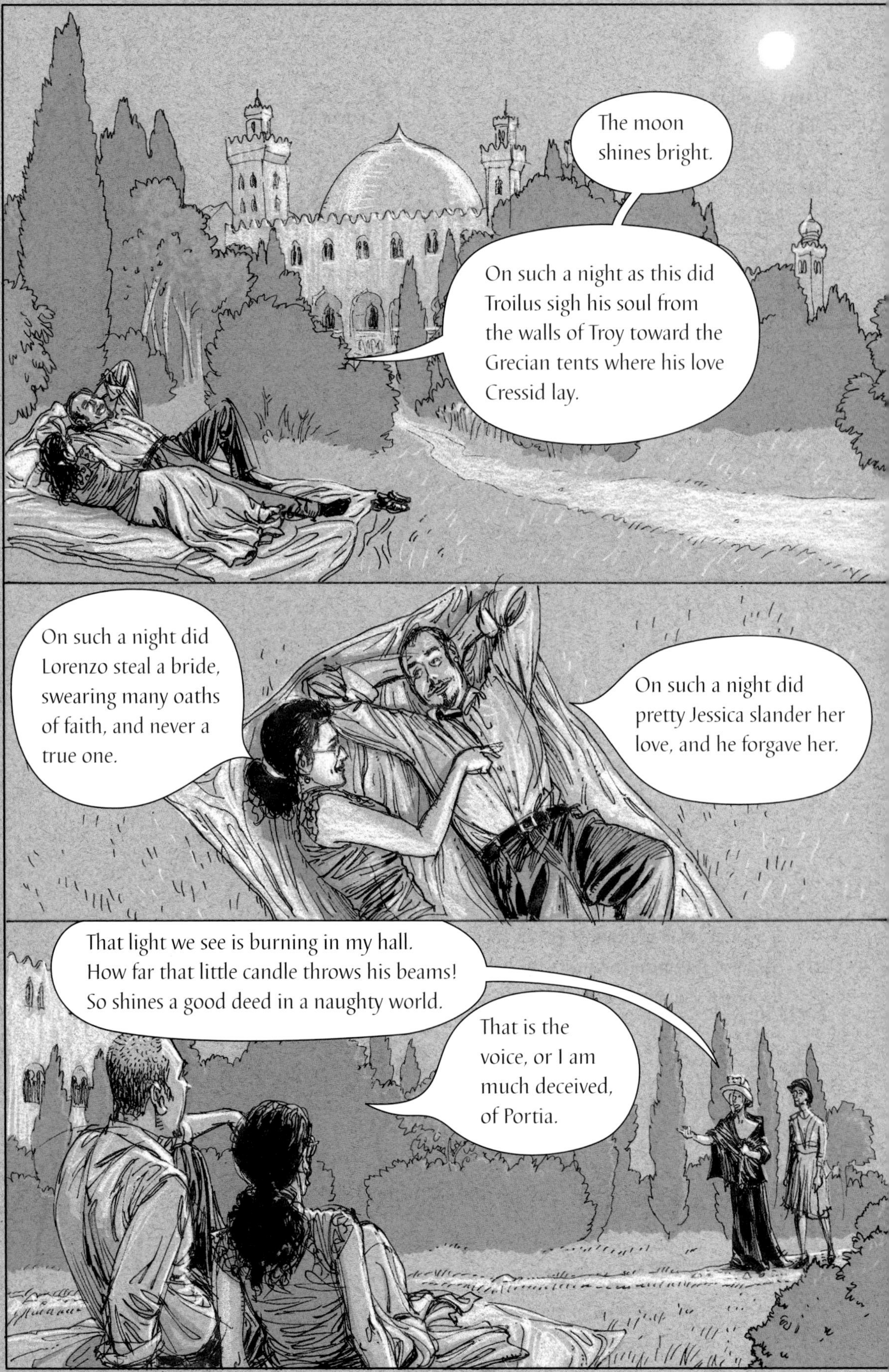
The moon shines bright.
On such a night as this did Troilus sigh his soul from the walls of Troy toward the Grecian tents where his love Cressid lay.
On such a night did Lorenzo steal a bride, swearing many oaths of faith, and never a true one.
On such a night did pretty Jessica slander her love, and he forgave her.
That light we see is burning in my hall. How far that little candle throws his beams! So shines a good deed in a naughty world.
That is the voice, or I am much deceived, of Portia.

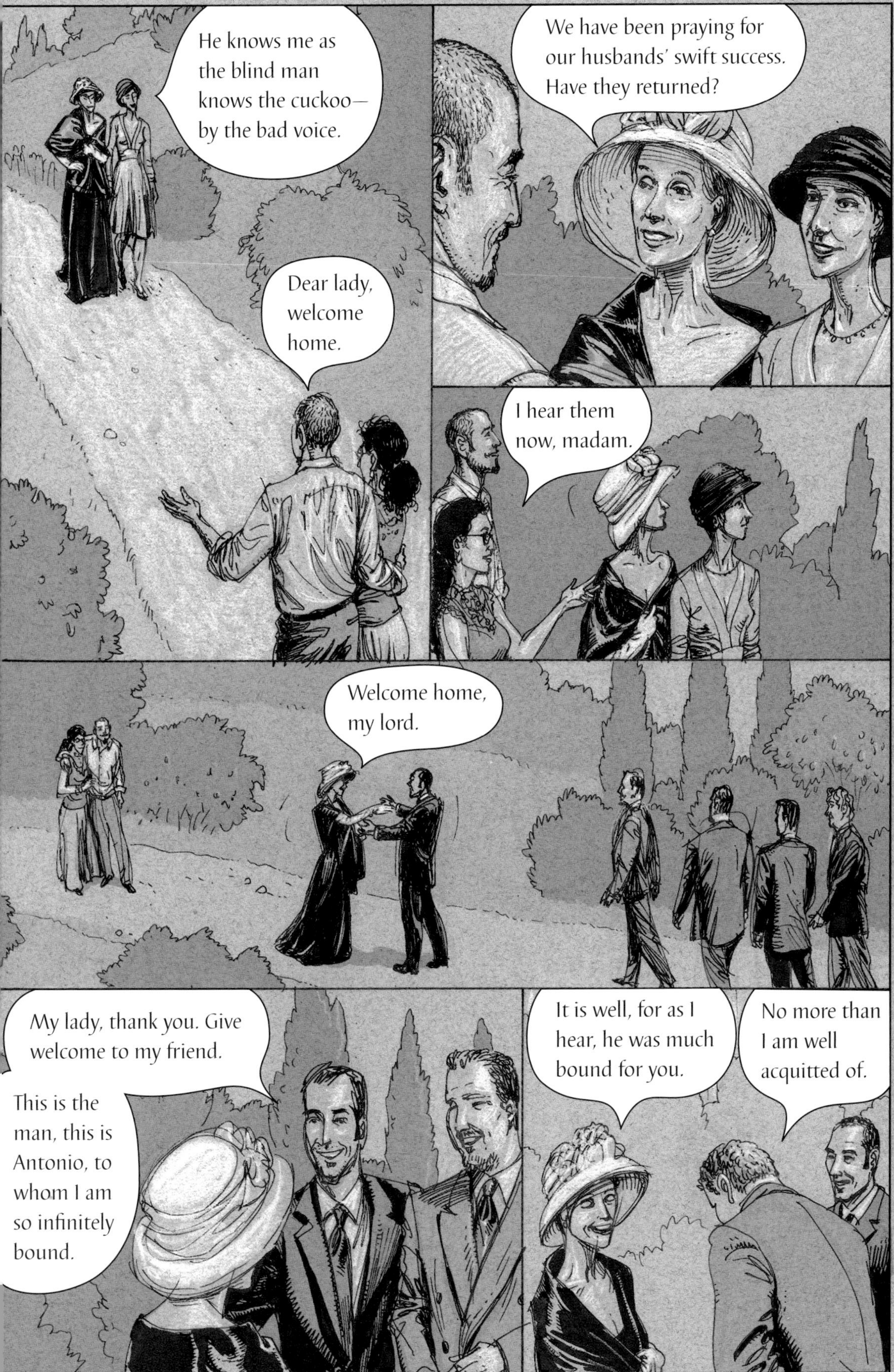
He knows me as the blind man knows the cuckoo—by the bad voice.
Dear lady, welcome home.
We have been praying for our husbands' swift success. Have they returned?
I hear them now, madam.
Welcome home, my lord.
My lady, thank you. Give welcome to my friend.
This is the man, this is Antonio, to whom I am so infinitely bound.
It is well, for as I hear, he was much bound for you.
No more than I am well acquitted of.

# AUTHOR'S NOTE

*The Merchant of Venice* is a controversial play. Was Shakespeare racist, or is the play a commentary on racism? Is it anti-Semitic or anti-Christian? What are we to make of the overtones of homosexuality? I am not going to take a position here, but if you are offended or intrigued by any aspect of the story, I encourage you to look further into these questions for yourself. There is a wealth of critical writing on them, and a simple Internet search will give you a good start.

More so than in my previous graphic novels, *Beowulf* and *King Lear*, my *Merchant* text is greatly altered from the original. A large amount of Shakespeare's material has been cut, including whole scenes and characters (such as the high-spirited Launcelot Gobbo and his aged father, depicted below), and many passages have been changed from verse to modern prose. However, when altering the sections that are still in verse, I made a strong effort to preserve the iambic pentameter and the feel of the language.

You may perceive a gradual shift through the course of the book from simpler, more modern prose to unedited Shakespearean verse. This is partly a sneaky way to get readers comfortable with the language, but mainly it is because the most famous speeches in this play occur near the end, in the court scene, and I wanted to preserve those in the original verse as much as possible.

I have chosen to set this book in a modern Venice. Staging Shakespeare in a modern setting is by no means a new idea. Many directors have done it to good effect, but it does inevitably create certain anachronisms, some trivial, some more jarring. In Shakespeare's time both anti-Semitism and slavery were commonplace. To the modern reader they seem alien (I hope). If you find them incongruous when placed in a modern setting, I urge you to consider that today we are still struggling with the same basic issue: man's inhumanity toward his fellow man.

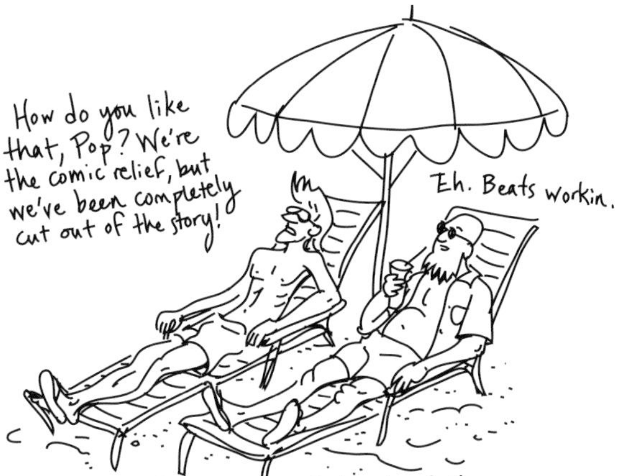
How do you like that, Pop? We're the comic relief, but we've been completely cut out of the story!
Eh. Beats workin.

# ACKNOWLEDGMENTS

I drew virtually all the characters in this book from models (posing live when possible, or else photographed). This was something I'd really been wanting to try, and it was a rewarding process despite the huge logistical challenges involved. All the models were my friends, or friends of friends, and I am enormously grateful to all of them for their good-natured hard work—especially the principal "actors," and most particularly "Saint Gayle" for her heroic patience through countless hours of posing as well as the horrors of dress shopping. Models, thank you all. Without you, this would have been a very different book.

| | |
|---|---|
| Antonio – **Paul Crook** | Jessica – **Melissa Marver** |
| Bassanio – **Gordon Fontaine** | Portia – **Gayle DeDe** |
| Gratiano – **Aaron Green** | Nerissa – **Theodora Van Roijen** |
| Salerio – **Salvador Casanas** | The Prince of Morocco – **Erick Quashie** |
| Salanio – **Edwin Maas** | The Prince of Aragon – **Kurt Bickenbach** |
| Lorenzo – **Juan Diaz** | The Duke of Venice – **Sean Hyde-Moyer** |
| Shylock (also Tubal) – **Don Davidoff** | Portia's servants/musicians – **Sarah Carrier** |

Additionally, for their assistance with the casting, I'd like to thank the Van Amsterdam family, Kelly Garvin, Kim Wutkiewicz, Wes Carroll, Mat MacKenzie, and Dianne Cowan. Mat and Diane also helped with early feedback on the script and layout, as did Joanne Greenberg and Paul Crook. Thanks also to Bruce Borham for his hospitality in Venice, Heather Glista for costume consulting, and Dave Merrill for Nerissa's manly hairstyle.

A very special thank-you to Alison Morris for constant support and help with casting, feedback, coloring, and a thousand other things.

I first read *Merchant* in a class at the New School under the outstanding instruction of Professor Arnold Klein. Preserved in the margins of my dog-eared copy of the play are many keen observations on the recurring themes and symbols in the play, and I thought I'd leave you with a small display of them—with all due credit and thanks to Mr. Klein.

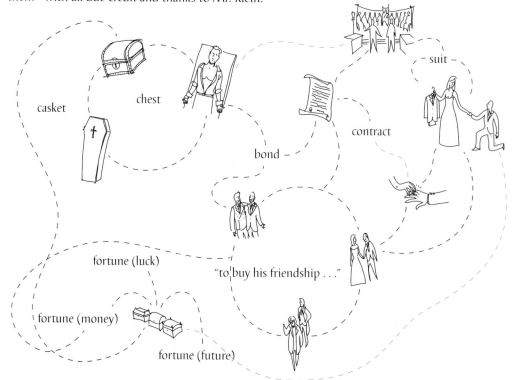

casket · chest · suit · contract · bond · fortune (luck) · "to buy his friendship . . ." · fortune (money) · fortune (future)

This is a work of fiction. Names, characters, places, and incidents are either products of the author's imagination or, if real, are used fictitiously.



First edition 2008

Library of Congress Cataloging-in-Publication Data is available.

Library of Congress Catalog Card Number 2007938349

ISBN 978-0-7636-3024-9

2 4 6 8 10 9 7 5 3 1

Printed in Singapore

This book was typeset in Barbedor.

Candlewick Press
2067 Massachusetts Avenue
Cambridge, Massachusetts 02140

visit us at www.candlewick.com

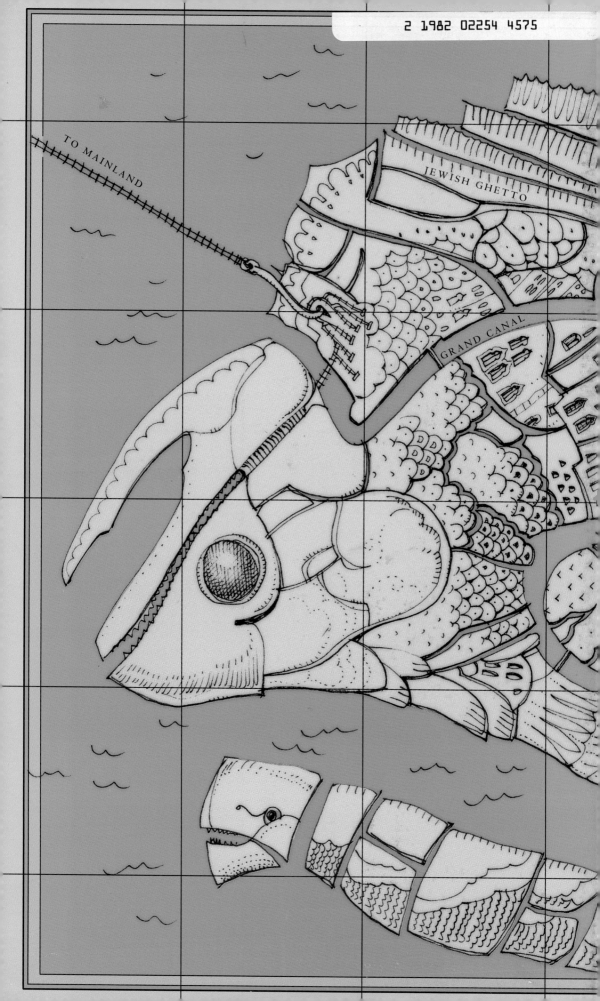

TO MAINLAND

JEWISH GHETTO

GRAND CANAL